The Nameless Tower

R.A.F. Klein

For my Cai Lun

Book One

I woke up in bonds, exhausted. The kind of tired felt only after battle: mind in a haze, body too weak to move. The rope around my wrists is mine; the dried blood of my friends is caked on the hemp. Laelia's blood, my blood. The tent over my head was put up fast. Trees leaned together to hold up a tired canvas. A tent of the Roman Legion far from its home. I know most of the men in here. Generals, some Roman, some Goth, they all look terrified. The slow burn of the setting sun is red on their faces, streaming in from the opening behind me. I turn to see the man to my right. It's hard to move my head, hard to find the will to do anything.

> *I just want to let go.*
> Bar-Abba. That giant of a man, it's his shadow over me.
> *How did I get here?*

Chapter 1

My nightmares jerk me out of sleep. I am still in the same cramped cell. I must have nodded off after a morning of torture.

Laelia's body lies across the prison hall. Her face still turned upward. Vitus will not stop pacing the room. The ice axe in his hand swings wildly with determination. The rest of Unit Seven awaits my order, immobile...or terrified. I count myself lucky. A peasant was not the man Rome wanted leading its army, but it's the man they got.

"Zeus, we need to get out of here. We *have* to run! Get up and do something!" Vitus yells over to me.

Why is he yelling so loud?

I cannot take my eyes off Laelia. Her mangled limbs and purple face. She looks like a dead dog left in the street.

"Zeus, please!"

Why does he keep yelling?

Laelia...this is all my fault. We should have never climbed this fucking mountain.

"Zeus?" Vitus pleads.

Fabius will not stop chuckling in the corner. "I can't believe they thought that was his name. Good memory, Vitus." He turns back to gnawing on a month old bone, savoring what is left of the marrow.

"████Try to focus, Fabius...please," Vitus says before turning back to me. "Jesus! Please get up."

It has been so long since anyone used that name. Dad called me that. Damn, I can't even remember his face now. Vitus is right, he always is.

"Sorry, Vitus, let's go," I say, jumping to attention and grabbing his axe to calm him.

I take off my coat, the only thing keeping me from freezing.

It should be strong enough to bend the iron bars.

Twisting the axe and leather to bend the cell door nearly dislocates my shoulder. With a snap of the axe, the bar shifts, just enough to slip through. Now we are down one ice tool. And I'm out a coat. If I get off this mountain, it will be a cold climb down.

"Vitus, relax. Cato, take point. Marcus, take flank. Fabius, you and I were always the slowest—we'll take the rear."

Fabius spits out the bone and jumps up to support me.

"These Neangri killed our friends. Let it go. We can't do anything about that now. We need to escape, not fight. If you kill one, do it quickly and silently. If they raise an alarm, we all die."

Cato, fists clenched, glances at Laelia, and puts on his coat. The rest do the same. We file out of our cell, careful not to disturb her body.

The wind bites down the moment we get outside. I wish I had that coat. Fields of deep snow, sheer cliffs of ice, and well crafted châlets surround us. The brilliant architecture of the Neangri belies their bloodlust. It is as if they are a torn race: living in peace in the mountains, yet thirsty for the destruction of man below.

We sprint through the village, making our way to the metal shop, not a single Neangri solider in sight. They had marched us along these paths many times. Then, the village was alive. Smoke rose from every glassy Chalet. Neangri soldiers glared at us as we passed. Now the village is dead.

Cato reaches the metal shop first. A hot ironworks sparks in the corner but no one is working it. Endless rows of weapons are spread before us. We take what we need and slip out as we entered.

Beyond the metal shop, their General's quarters sits atop the summit of Khan Tengri. From the metal shop to the top is a stadium's length at most. A short climb compared to the distance we climbed to get here.

The moment we step out, a piercing bell chimes. Cato launches out onto the snowfield toward the summit. Vitus, Marcus, and Fabius follow. I pause and turn around out of morbid curiosity. A teeming horde of dispassionate Neangri load their weapons behind us. Fear, anger, hatred, all of these emotions are absent from our enemy, only duty remains. The task of our execution. Cato was right. We had to run.

Tiny metal shards fly past our heads, each followed by a loud blast. Iron and fire lap at our heels. Thunder bursts at our ears. With each shot the Neangri grow closer to hitting their mark.

Vitus takes up his sword in one hand and his ice axe in the other, using them as climbing tools as he claws up the mountain. Marcus throws his body upwards, tossing his weight like a leap frog.

"Fabius, Vitus, Cato! Did you ever expect *this* when we met that skinny little Jew?" Marcus asks. A tiny shard barely misses its mark and lands at Marcus's toe just as he jumps.

Cato launches up like a jackrabbit, his breathing heavy. Another shard lands near his shoulder. We know the Neangri well. They are on top of us but their movement is silent.

"Marcus, really? Can you shut up? You'll give away our position," Cato says.

"Give away our position? Do you think they forgot we're here?" Vitus calls back ahead of us. "A fight was inevitable, and we all know how you love a fight!"

Fabius, a hair's breadth from my heels, claws his way up the snow. He grunts at his friend's blithe indifference in this situation. I turn to check on him. A Neangri grabs his ankle and pulls hard, ruthless dispassion in its eyes. He kicks hard and climbs on.

To our right, several milliaria below, an endless ocean of peaks, timeless glaciers snaking between them, carving new cliffs as they make their slow march toward the sea. Behind us, the sun rises above the Neangri horde, momentarily blotting them out and lighting up the mountain in an amaranth glow. The horde closes in.

My focus returns as my axe slips and I stumble backwards. I pull my knife and plunge it in the ice. One axe was not how I wanted to climb today.

Shrapnel misses Marcus by a hair, slamming into the snowpack, shards of ice cutting his face. He climbs on.

We reach the top of the couloir with metal snapping at our heels. The five of us vault over the summit lip in unison, landing softly in the deep snow on the other side.

My stomach shoots into my throat. Our mistake is instantly obvious. Twenty Neangri stand before us, their weapons aimed. They could have shot us while we climbed. They waited until we were so close to victory. A hail of metal rushes past my ears. The soft sound of bodies falling to snow billows up from both sides. A splatter of wet heat hits me in the face. Fabius lies face down, right next to me. I wipe my cheek. It's blood—the last Seven had to give. The rage I have hidden my entire life boils over. One guttural cry escapes, strong enough to frighten even the Neangri. I sprint past them, knocking one out cold with a high knee to the face.

In blind fury, I kick in the doors and leap onto the back of the first Neangri I find, wrapping my hands around his throat. The beast is unfazed. He slowly turns around. As if my hands are a trinket around his neck, he peels me from his back, and tosses me against a wall like a rag doll. The blow knocks out what little wind is left in my body.

I look up into his face contorting and shifting with the fire light. The man I have sought my whole life stares back. A smile stretches his scarred face. In my native tongue, he calmly speaks to awaiting soldiers: "Fetch the rope…"

My mind hazes. A single thought booms.

Bar-Abba?

Chapter 2

"I grew up poor. When I was twelve, I guess that makes it seven years now, I watched a Roman platoon slaughter thirty Jewish protestors in the street. Judea is an awful place."

This bar is filthy, and this beer…

"Hey! This beer tastes like piss," I yelled over the bar keeper.

"Zeus!" he yelled back. "Who the hell are you talking to? We've all heard your story, so keep it to yourself."

The Babak was filthy, as always. It was about three in the morning and I was drunk, drunker than most nights. I'd been on the road for over a year now, far away from my home, far away from that man.

This bar was much like every other I had been in, always in the most whore-ridden neighborhoods. When you spend so long on the road, the nuances begin to bleed together. Roughly hewn tables and chairs of scrap crudely sanded to create a surface to sit on. Floors of dirt, stained with countless nights of abuse, often semen. Of course the Babak had a nasty bar keeper, overweight and foul-mouthed, also often covered in dried semen (I hoped his own). This was not the kind of place anyone would want to whittle away the hours in, but I often did.

My beer was warm, stale, and weak. All I wanted to do was forget, but all the alcohol in Seleucia was not going to cut it.

Shit! I need to get out of here.

"Zeus." The bar keeper nudged me and I pulled my head from deep out of the bar top.

"What?" I slurred.

He hit me over the head with a wooden cup. "That man over there bought you another drink, something stronger; try to not be a little shit. Stupid Jew fuck…." The last part was mumbled but even drunk I could hear him.

I took the glass and held it up in thanks to the only other person at the bar. He had a hood on over his face and the rest of him was strangely dressed. He walked over and sat next to me, careful not to show his face.

"I've never heard your story. But I have to ask, what are you doing here?"

I downed the drink in one gulp. My mind hazed in an instant. It was strong, too strong.

12

"Thanks stranger," I said. My words were thick and slow, sap from a tree. "If you have to pry, I'm here because the man I hate most isn't. This is as far as I could make it from him, and what he did."

The stranger shifted his seat. Flickers of candle light caught on the features of his face beneath the hood. He was white, bearded, and had green eyes. My drink clouded the rest.

"Who's that?" he asked.

"Well," I hiccupped and threw my arms over the bar top, trying to make a comfortable place to put my head. "He raped my mom and my girlfriend too. Though the second might have been transactional."

Shit that drink was strong. The room needs to stop spinning.

"I'm sorry to hear that. Zeus was it?" he asked, trying hard to be sympathetic. Strangers never really care though. They are all out for something.

"What do you want?" I asked. "Why the free drink?" I couldn't make his face out anymore. The whole room was spinning and getting darker.

"Just trying to be kind," he said. "Where are you from?" I banged my head hard on the bar top, trying to clear my senses. "A hole outside Judea. A tiny fishing village no one cares about." I looked up, but the room was still moving. Faster and faster.

Right then, as if on cue, Khshayarsha walked in. He had two whores, one on each arm. A black one with her tits hanging out, and one with olive skin. The lighter skinned one was young, and she looked like it was her first time. Khshayarsha had her in a headlock when he came stumbling in. He was an awful man, a Goliath and the spitting image of Hercules. More cock than man really, evidenced by the tandem whores.

"Beer for my two friends Canor!" he yelled over to the bar man.

Canor gave him a large bottle and backed off. Khshayarsha had some seedy connections and most of the city knew to stay clear of him. I hated the man; we had gotten into more than a few fights. He reminded me of *him*.

"Friend of yours?" the stranger asked noticing the angst on my face.

Whatever was in that drink made me furious, frothing, as if all the walking I did to get out of Judea, to get away from *him*, meant nothing. Khshayarsha was just as bad, maybe worse, and his whore looked like her, like Mary.

Shit!

I shot out of my chair, crashing it to the ground, and stumbled over to Khshayarsha.

"You filthy fuck pig!" I yelled. "You have to bring those things in here?" I pointed to the two whores. The younger blushed and tried to hide her face.

Khshayarsha laughed, guttural and throaty. "The little Jew wants us to get out, girls." He leaned over and licked the black ones breast, staring right into my eyes as he tongue fucked her ebony nipple.

"Get out!" My rage boiled over. All I could think about was Mary, the woman I was supposed to spend the rest of my life with. I saw her, her and Bar-Abba, fucking slowly in the back alleys of my town. Mary's ramshackle lean-to the only thing keeping their sinful act a secret. Without thinking I grabbed the olive skin whore, threw her to the dirt and kicked Khshayarsha hard in the shin.

He threw the black whore aside, and pulled a knife.

"You two stop!" Canor yelled. "You keep at it and I'm getting the guards. It's too early for this!"

Neither of us was in the mood for reason. Canor sprinted out of the bar, leaving us to our violence. I'd been on the road for a while, been in plenty of scraps, half of them with this very man, but the drink the stranger gave me made it impossible to see straight. I was on the ground in seconds, Khshayarsha's foul, cum stained hands at my throat. I could smell his sweat, his face was so close I could feel the beard hairs tickle my chin. With a pungent stroke, he licked my face like a dog and held the knife to my throat.

"I've been waiting to do this for a long time, you nasty Jew son of a bitch. Where do you want to get fucked first?" He pushed the knife hard into my cheek as he breathed down my face. I could feel hot blood dripping.

The stranger came over from behind us, calm and steady. I could hear his footfall and make out his boots before Khshayarsha even noticed. With one hard kick, the stranger knocked Khshayarsha out cold. The two whores ran, screaming from the bar and two guards came rushing in after them. Canor pointed to me and Khshayarsha, and we were in irons before I was off the ground.

"See you soon, Zeus," the stranger said, as the guards led us out of the Babak.

14

All in all, a standard night for a nineteen year old in Seleucia.

The moment my face hit the sand in the prison cell I passed out. The drink the stranger gave me was the strongest I ever had. I fell into a restless sleep and dreamt of my time as a child.

I dreamt of my mother's face, something I sorely missed, and of my friends: Hermes and Mary. We had been together for years, shared everything. Until I left that day.

Hermes was the same age as me, and the only boy I got along with. He wasn't really Greek, only jealous of my nickname so Hermes just stuck. He was the kind of kid who always found trouble, a conspirator. But he was brilliant. I think we got along because we couldn't stand what was happening in our town. Rome moved in with harsh whips and swift executions. It made us angry, and it made us friends.

Mary was beautiful; I loved her from the start. We first met in the rock pools just north of town. Hermes and I played there all the time. I found Mary washing her face in one of the shallow basins.

When I was eleven, Mary led us deep into the desert wasteland. She brought a braided cord she'd stolen from a laundry line. We left early, sneaking out past our snoring parents. That time of day the desert is cold. Hermes brought a small loaf of bread for us to share, and I brought the tea to keep us warm. When Hermes and I went into the desert we always stopped at those shallow pools. Mary pressed on, further than we had ever been, another two hours walk outside our comfort.

We stopped only when Mary did. The flat wasteland had turned into rocky pillars. We found a sheer cliff of beautiful sandstone. That cliff could not have been more than thirty spans. A span was about two Roman pedes or about the height of a small child—but to Hermes and I, it seemed higher than a cloud.

The cliff was a deep crimson marred with large swaths of black—smooth to the touch but not featureless. A fissure split the cliff, no more than two fingers wide. About a third of the way up a large roof capped the wall, the width of a man. I recall thinking how impossible of an obstacle a roof like that would be. I was no skilled climber, but Hermes and I had shared a few mishaps on trees and small boulders. Clearing over this jutting prow would require a brave soul. I imagined a climber jumping up the wall to gain the ledge over the roof, the only other option I could think of was to fly.

When we reached the cliff base, Mary slipped off her sandals, wrapped the cord around her waist and started to climb. I guessed I would see a brave soul fly today.

Mary led out onto the bust of the cliff with relative ease. She fished her nimble fingers into the sharp crack and suspended her weight from them. Her feet stuck to the smooth stone as she smeared them up the wall. We had never seen a girl do what she dared, not even a grown man.

When she reached the roof she took a brief rest.

"Are you two afraid of a little stone?" she said, glaring at us from her perch.

Hermes and I just stood there, staring dumbly up as she jammed both hands in the crack atop the roof. With one wild scream she pulled herself over the bulge and out onto the exposed face. Within moments, she was at the top looking down on us, triumphantly catching her breath.

As I watched Mary that day, it became clear that the strength of this girl was to be admired. I loved her more than I could bear.

We made the long walk home. The mid-day sun scorched our backs, but I kept my sweaty hand in Mary's the whole time.

The dream cleared, like a morning fog, another replaced it. Bar-Abba... I saw him and Mary, in her lean-to hut. His hands around her throat, eyes bulging as she gasped for air, clawed at his back. He stared me down as I stood at the entrance to the alley, helpless, useless. He thrust himself into her, harder and harder, her face growing purple from the pressure. I tried to run to help her, help my wife, but my legs were cemented to the earth. I cried, and in a flash Bar-Abba's hands were around my throat. They were so large, so strong. My breath gave out.

I shot awake,coughing.

When I opened my eyes, Khshayarsha face was there to greet me. He was squatting in the corner of the cell, shitting into a cathole. His face was red from the exertion.

"Those two whores cost me..." he paused for a hard push and then breathed a sigh of exquisite relief. "Ten pieces of silver. Who's gonna pay Jew?"

I woke up slow, despite the stench, and sat up. "Khshayarsha, it's not my fault they ran away screaming." I took a moment to rub my eyes and breathed through my mouth. The last thing I wanted was any of his odor getting in my nose. "They probably would have run away screaming

16

anyway if you got them to bed."

He jiggled his backside a few times and stood up. We both had chains around our ankles and hands, forcing him to waddle over. The scene would have been comical if I didn't know this man wanted to kill me.

"What did you say?" he asked, so close I could smell his breath.

I recoiled instinctively. He smelled like rotting meat. "How old was the younger one Khshayarsha? Twelve, thirteen? You're a sick fuck, you know that?"

He gave me one swift knee to the face, and sat back down. It hurt, but not as much as my headache. I was hung-over. Worse than I'd ever been.

We sat in silence for a while, at opposite ends of the cell. It was a bar fight we were in for and it shouldn't have been more than a few hours before the guards let us out.

After about a day, I got worried. Half way through that night, a guard came and moved us into different cells. They were tired of our quarrelling, but no one released us. I didn't steal a thing, neither did Khshayarsha, as far as I knew; we both should have been out of there by now.

It was a few days before I found out what was going on. It turned out Khshayarsha was wanted. Everyone knew he was in a gang. I think Mithradates was the leader. But no one ever did anything about it. As it turned out, there was a new head guard in Seleucia, and he was eager to get rid of Mithradates and his men. I, having been in the wrong place at the wrong time, was suspected as being a part of this gang.

After a week, a young child was thrown into the cell with me. He didn't talk for two days, didn't move, didn't even get up to piss.

I had to pick the locks off his feet before he would trust me, a trick I learned working as a carpenter when I was young. Splinters have many uses besides irritating the skin.

"Thank you," he said, as quiet as the rats around us.

"What's your name?" I asked.

"Jude... Do you have anything to eat?"

He looks a little like Hermes. I missed my friend.

"Jude, huh. You remind me of a friend I had when I was young. Short for Judas right? Are you from Hebron?" I tore off half the bread I was hiding in my robes and handed it to the boy. He gulped it down in

17

one mouthful so I gave him the rest.

"Yes," he said, stale bread spilling out. "You look Jewish too."

"Once," I answered, happy to have a civil conversation again. "Now I'm not so sure. But I am from that area. My friends call me Zeus."

Jude laughed a little. "I thought you said you were Jewish?"

"It's a long story, just something my mom used to call me I guess. I try not to use my name on the road too much. Most the people out here hate Jews. I think I could pass for Greek." I pulled up my sleeve and flexed, mimicking Adonis. "What do you think?"

Jude laughed again. "Not even close." He looked around the cell like a mouse, "do you have any more food?"

I shook my head. "That was it. They feed us once a day so you will have to wait until tomorrow. Sorry buddy."

"What are you in for?" he asked.

"You know Jude, I'm not entirely sure. You?"

"Stealing food from the city market."

I shook my head in disbelief. "That'll do it."

I'd been in that cell for a while now, and it felt good to talk again. I stood up and started scouring the room for small stones with a great idea in mind.

"You know Jude, when I was about your age; I got really good at a Roman game. My mom taught it to me."

"Yeah?" he said with delight. "Which one?"

"Lantrunculi, ever heard of it?"

"Ha!" he blurted out. "Yeah, I know it."

"Oh yeah? Actually, there are about fifty pieces of silver waiting for me when I get out of here. You know how I got so much?"

He shook his head.

I picked up the last of thirty one little stones. "By playing!" And dropped them on the ground in front of Jude.

He caught on immediately and traced out a makeshift board in the sand.

The sandy cell floor became a grid, spaces *a-h* horizontally, and 1-8 vertically. I gave Jude sixteen of the stones and took fifteen for myself. Lantrunculi was a remarkably simple game, but took decades to master. Each player has sixteen pieces on their side of the board. The white player on a1 and a2 through h1 and h2, black four spaces away, opposite. Each piece could move a certain direction on the board, though some players made their own rules. The only piece that mattered was the dux: lose that, and the game was over. When I was ten, mom had given me a special dux. It was pure silver and worth more than a house. A fitting piece for the one that matters most. Lantrunculi was about strategy but it was also about reading your opponent. I could tell Jude knew this, his face blanked as soon as he set his pieces.

"Where is your dux?" he asked.

I pulled my family heirloom from deep within my robes. I kept it with me all the time, the only piece of home I had left. "Right here," I said, holding it up.

I placed the dux on my favored position, and Jude on his. Jude was on the far side, meaning he was white, so I let him go first. After a moment of thought, he made his first move: pawn out two spaces, d4.

As I moved my piece out, carefully evaluating his face, Jude asked "What are you doing in Seleucia, Zeus?"

The face of Mary shot into my mind. I mirrored Jude's move, pawn straight out, d5. "I wasn't too fond of what Judea was turning into. So I left."

He grabbed a pawn and idly played with it. "I know what you mean. My mother died giving birth to me, my father a few years before that. My grandfather took care of me for a while, but then the Romans killed him." His second pawn moved out to flank his previous, c4.

That's strange. Maybe a coincidence?
I thought about what I saw when I was young. The scene was still so fresh in my mind, six years ago but it seemed like yesterday.

"I'm sorry Jude."

Wait! Why did he move his pawn there? I could take it and free up the board for any development I wanted. His face was blank; if he had planned this gambit, it was not showing.

"When I was thirteen," I started to tell the story I told almost every night when I was drunk. "I watched a Roman platoon slaughter a would-be mob. My friends and I went to see a preacher, and he would not shut up about Marcus Ambivius."

I took his pawn, dxc4, while I continued my story.

"The preacher worked the crowd up and the Romans moved in with decisive action. They killed most of the people there. My friends and I ran before it got really bad. Right before I left, I watched a soldier kill an old man and crush his baby in the street. Strange coincidence, don't you think?"

He moved again, unstirred by the loss of his piece, e3. He was paying more attention to my story than the game. "How long ago was this?"

"Six years." I threw my solider onto the board with a slam, three spaces down and one right, f6. "How old are you?"

"Eight." He still wasn't looking. His priest slithered up diagonally to my pawn, fxc4.

My pawn! How did I miss that?

We paused and looked at each other in disbelief.

I moved my pawn to e6, a timid move. The mood silenced us both and I was afraid I brought up some terrible memories for my friend. "I didn't mean to..."

Jude groaned and moved his own soldier to f3. "I don't need your sympathy."

This boy is smart, and strong.

"I guess you really have played before, little buddy," I said. He was still distracted; I could see him trying to keep tears from welling up. I moved with a little more courage and set up a ruse of my own. My pawn to c5, he would have to take the piece.

Jude castled his dux, protecting it in the back at g1. *Was he scared?* I moved another pawn to a6, giving me time to evaluate his strategy.

"How did you make it out here all on your own?" I asked.

He advanced another pawn to e4, apparently as an answer.

Now we were just toying with each other, weighing the other's moves.

He sat for a few moments, maybe thinking about what I asked, maybe trying not to cry. Whatever his story was, it was sadder than mine. I felt guilty for wallowing in self pity for over a year.

A flurry of moves followed before an answer came. Our secret war spilled out onto the board, and it became clear that Jude was not distracted at all, merely luring me in for the kill.

My pawn to b5 answered his last move. He wouldn't even look at me anymore. There was an intense concentration in his face, one masking a great internal pain.

Jude's priest to d3, mine to b7. His to g5, letting me take a pawn, cxd4. His soldier took my pawn in retaliation, fxd4. Move after move, we traded piece for piece. Jude's face turned red hot, he was almost frothing. Fourteen exchanges later we each had seven of the other's pieces. I had never seen a child play like this. He calmed and the silence lifted.

"I don't know… luck I guess," he said. His face was now calm.

"Very lucky indeed."

My dux was in the open at f8; he could take it in two moves.

He moved his queen in front of his well-guarded dux instead of setting me up for the kill. "I've always been lucky. Some other children found me when I was two. They said I was lying in a gutter, covered in blood. It was right after a fight."

"Really?" I asked. The game was getting close, too close.

The last move sealed my fate; our duxes were facing each other, mine at g6, and his at g1.

"The kids I grew up with taught me how to survive, at any cost. It seems like you know what that takes."

"I do…"

Neither of us moved, on the board nor to make eye contact after the aggressive play.

"You're a Jew and you hide it. I'm a thief and I hide it. Well at least I try to." He seemed so wise, so astute for an eight year old. I suppose life is the real teacher, and this kid had lived a lot in his short time.

At first Jude wouldn't look at the board, now he wouldn't look at me.

A guard came to our cell door, and slammed his staff on the iron bars. He was furious at us for playing. Behind him was a tall man, hooded and cloaked. It was the same cloak I saw in the Babak over a week ago. The stranger who gave me that drink. He stopped the guard before his anger boiled over, grabbing his staff and breaking it in one swift move.

"Zeus?" he asked through the bars. "Who's your friend?"

The guard started to yell, even more furious this man had broken his staff. In another flurry of moves the stranger twisted the guard, slammed him against the cell door, and held his hand over his mouth.

"I paid you your silver," the stranger said, calm and reverent considering the situation. "Let this man out."

The guard coughed in acquiescence, and reached around for his key.

"And," the stranger continued, putting more pressure on the guards face. "If you want to keep your arm, I'd let out the boy too."

The door fell open with a clang and Jude and I jumped up to greet our savior. Jude sprinted out like a hare; he saw an opportunity and took it. That's what survival is for most of us. Before leaving, I ran back to our sandy game, I didn't want to leave my silver dux.

I looked at the board to see how close I was to losing. Jude's dux was gone and mine was the only piece left. I took it and I walked out. I didn't see the boy again.

The stranger had already vanished when I made it outside.

Why was this man following me?

I spent a few hours looking for my little buddy. I wanted to help him out, and I had the money to do it. But no one I asked had ever heard of him.

After sunset I went back to the Babak. Canor kept my silver and my latrunculi board for me. He was the closest thing to a friend you could have in a city like this. I spent so many nights there because I spent so many evenings playing the game I had become a master at. Underground latrunculi betting was popular in the city, and I was one of the best. The game with Jude was a strange fluke, and I had never gotten anywhere near that close to losing since I moved out here from Judea.

But that night there were no players, only drunks.

Canor greeted me with surprise when I entered, like nothing had happened. "Zeus! My old friend! Welcome back."

I gave him a half hearted smile and sat at the bar.

"I wasn't sure you'd make it out this time," he said. "I heard they thought you were in Mithradates' gang with Khshayarsha. Now a word to the wise." He came over and poured me a beer, then grabbed me by my shirt. "You keep that shit out of my bar."

I could smell his unwashed mouth, and what had been in it. I didn't even want to think about where his mouth had been.

"You come in here every night," he continued. "Get drunk, tell your same stories and start fights. No more! You do it again and I'll make sure you don't make it out of jail next time."

At that he let me go and I plopped back into my seat. I picked up my cup and drained it. I was already too listless to care anymore.

"You still have my silver?" I asked.

Canor laughed. "Barely. I was about to sell it you were gone so long." He handed over my sack and I guessed the weight. "It's all there. And here's your board too."

He meant my custom latrunculi set. I had paid twenty pieces for it and pulled it out of his hands jealously.

"That stranger was looking for you again," Canor said. "Told me he'd be back tonight. Who is that guy?"

I shrugged and held up my cup for more. Canor obliged. He was good at keeping me drunk.

Around the same time as before, the hooded stranger showed up. Late in the morning, and far into my drunkenness. I was passed out on the bar top when he woke me up.

Dreams of Bar-Abba again, always Bar-Abba.

This time the stranger had his cloak off. He was tan, muscular, and looked Greek. A tight mop of curls on his head, but a thin beard on his face.

"Who are you?" I asked. "What do you want with me?"

He practically picked me up out of the chair and led me out back. The alley behind the Babak was for whores and their work. The thin walkway was lined with them, a few with customers. I vomited immediately. The smell of sex was overpowering. It took me a few minutes before I could stand back up and stomach it.

"You done?" the stranger asked.

I coughed a little and shook my head. "You want to answer my questions?"

He took me to a space on the wall, not occupied with people fucking, and we sat down.

"Cai Lun," he said.

"OK, Cai Lun. Now what do you want with me?"

"We will get to that."

A dark skinned whore came over and pulled up her skirt. "You two wanna spin?"

Cai Lun shot her an impetuous look. His green eyes were commanding. She dropped her skirt and walked away without a word.

"This city is awful," he said. "How can you stand it here?"

"I can't, to be honest, but it's better than home."

"Where's that?" he asked.

Didn't we have this conversation?

"It's been a while, and I was drunk both times, but I feel like I already told you this," I said. "Not to be rude."

"You told me," he recounted, " 'some shit town no one cares about.' Based on your accent I'd say north of Jerusalem. And based on your skin, I'd say a desert."

"That's very good," I laughed. "Most people can pick out a Jew though. But that's not who I am."

He spun around in a flash and squatted in front of me. His eyes were so piercing, yet his gaze so calm. "So who are you?"

I'm not sure...

"I guess I never thought about it Cai Lun. Give me a few weeks to answer, yeah?" I chuckled and stood up. "Now if you don't mind, I've been in jail for a week, and I'd like a good night's rest. Thanks for bailing me out by the way."

I turned to leave, and he was in front of me before I realized it. With one twist he threw me to the ground and pinned me with his knee. I tried to fight out of instinct; I was a survivor like Jude. Cai Lun was strong, fast, and forceful. I couldn't move.

He leaned in close. "Most men have forgotten what it means to care for something greater than themselves. You might want to think on that when you finally come up with an answer."

"Get the fuck off me!" I turned my head and screamed. By the time the words came out he was gone.

The same dark skin whore came back over, this time her top off. "I'll get the fuck on you!"

I spat and walked away.

What was Cai Lun's problem? Why me?

Damn, I need to sleep.

I thought about what he asked. Who was this random stranger to make me question who I was? I'm a survivor. I left my home because I was afraid, afraid of Bar-Abba, afraid of becoming my father and living that life, afraid of what it meant to stay under Roman rule. So I ran away. Why should a man stick around when there is nothing but fear? A survivor runs.

Bar-Abba was in Judea, so I couldn't be.

I poured myself into latrunculi for what seemed like a lifetime. Fifty pieces of silver turned into eighty, then into two hundred. I did the right thing leaving. Seleucia was where I was supposed to be, I knew it.

When I set out from my home, the world was shifting. Rome was gaining control over all the lands I knew. The sparse kingdoms that threatened her were growing further apart and more desperate. Some traders that made their way through Seleucia talked about an empire even greater, the Han they called it. But it was so far away it seemed like a legend. It made my choice to move into Seleucia all the more right.

It seemed the world wanted me to forget everything about Judea, about Bar-Abba, and about myself.

It was three months since I saw that stranger, since he drugged me and beat me in the alley. Now it was only a bitter memory.

Three in the morning again, but this time the Babak was alive. I was at the tail end of an eight-hour stint of play. I was at the top of my game, my latrunculi moves were unbeatable. And I had just taken down another opponent, adding five pieces of silver to my stack.

Cai Lun walked in, no hood, no cloak, only determination on his face. He noticed my silver and shot to the table. I looked up when I caught him pausing half way there. He weighed and measured me with his gaze, careful to stop on my eyes.

I darted back and forth between his penetrating gaze and his red silken robe, lavishly decorated with gold figures of lions, ravens, and dragons. The lacquered, black embroidery matched his beard. He would not stop stroking the hairs; it seemed unsanitary and haughty, given the environment.

He bowed slowly when he reached the table. "Zeus, pleasure to see you again. Would I be able to play you next?"

His Pahlavanik was perfect this time, no accent, articulate and the enigma had vanished.

He pulled out the chair of the man I had just beaten, sending him smacking to the ground.

"Hey, fuckhead!" the drunk local screamed.

"Líkāi zhèlǐ," Cai Lun roared back.

His tone commanded respect, but his cadence made it obvious that he had spent many years taming a vicious temper. At first I stood to object, but the return of his stabbing green eyes sat me down like a well trained mutt.

"Sorry, I break into Han Chinese when I get perturbed." He returned to Pahlavanik. "Do you speak Latin, friend?"

I was sure this man wasn't my friend. "No, Cai Lun, I do not. And keep your hands away from my drink!"

My drunk, used-to-be friend staggered out, and Cai Lun took his place.

"This backwards language it is." He took the stones on the board and rearranged them in a practiced and methodical order. I could tell it was time to concentrate, and possibly earn respect if I was to walk out of there with any of my winnings.

"Your parents must have been very prudent to so thoroughly educate their son," I said with an obvious air of reverence. "Three languages? Impressive."

Cai Lun rolled his eyes. "No need to bootlick. I would rather see how you play."

I had played as white all night, it was my lucky color and I had made enough money to make sure my personal set of lantrunculi stones were as polished and pure as Roman marble. Now, when I looked down at my set, they had turned jet black. They were my stones for sure; I had bought the marble and had a stone mason carve the figures. I knew them well. My soldiers looked like little Roman Legionnaires, and my Priests looked like Zoroastrian holy men. They were my stones, but now they were black.

What was going on?

Cai Lun's first move, pawn to e4, was standard and rational. I didn't question it, and I didn't think it wise to show any confusion over my pieces.

I moved a pawn to c6 and made doubly sure my dux was in place. The small ball of silver was the only memory of my mother.

What was this man's secret?

They way he spoke grew on me quickly. It was like a scolding father, and a sympathetic lover. Not that I knew anything about sympathy from my lovers. Our previous encounters had been marked by inebriation, so perhaps I had never noticed.

"To respond to your adulation, my parents were no more prudent than any other. They were concerned citizens in a time of Roman gentrification. Happy to have a son, but happier still to dream of a free government. I spent my youth baking mostly."

A baker? He moved his pawn to d4.

"Really?" I asked. "Yet you were able to learn three languages?" I moved my pawn to d5, setting him up for a gambit I made as a child.

"Six," he corrected. His soldier to c3. "My theory about excessive praise is that it weakens the mind and dulls the senses."

Well I guess my ruse didn't work. I took his pawn, dxe4.

"Six languages?" His solider took my pawn, cxe4.

How did he take that? How did I miss that?! I tried to control the look of shock on my face.

26

He smiled, not in secret. There was no need for this man to mask his emotions in this place. I moved my solider out to d7.

"When I was about your age," he looked at me close, "Achaea became a hot bed." He moved his soldier to g5. "Things got worse and worse, until I finally couldn't take it anymore and left."

I moved a second soldier out to f6. *No use playing coy.*

"And you have learned six languages since?" I asked.

His priest danced out to d3 before he began staring into my soul again. "Are you trying to distract me…sorry I never caught your name? Because I am sure it is not really Zeus."

Time to move slow. I couldn't figure out his next move, pawn to e6.

Cai Lun kept staring and my mind began to haze. I was tired, true, but now I felt drunk.

What power did he have? I've had my hand on my drink from the moment I saw him step in.

I took a sip of my beer; it was cold but bitter enough to refocus my mind.

Too bitter.

His solider went to f3. We both had most of our pieces in play. This was not the time for uncertainty, but I could not lift the veil of confusion from my mind.

"Well you certainly aren't Greek so I won't be using that name anymore. I heard Tiberius," he continued, still staring at me, "the Roman Tiberius has made Greece an Imperial state, and that conditions have improved since I left. It's been so long I cannot find the heart to care."

I moved my far pawn out to h6. The move was weak but I couldn't think of what else to do.

What was in my beer?!

"What do you do now?" I asked.

His solider took my pawn, hxe6.

My queen is exposed!

Cai Lun was still staring at me.

"I did work for the emperor of the Han. As it turns out, that type of job is not as stable as I thought."

My queen!

I had to think fast but everything moved slowly, as if in honey.

"Emperor Ping," he continued. "That was who I used to work for. And those that preceded him did not have beliefs; they had ideas.

Wang Mang…Sorry—friend, are you going to move?"

He didn't wait for me to answer before moving my own piece and protecting my queen at e7.

"As I was saying," his smile widened as the room began to spin. "Wang Mang, the new Han despot, believes that he has been sent by a deity. His methods and his zealous beliefs are dangerous."

"How can a belief be dangerous?" I heard my words slur as they vomited out of my mouth, a slow trickle of immature spittle from my stupefied mind.

Cai Lun took to stroking his beard and castled his dux. "A belief in religion, in a higher ideal that one cannot understand creates a way of behaving that fits each situation. A person with a belief, a pedagogical dogma—is a belief that is understood as true but is not empirically understood. Passing knowledge in this method does not promote understanding. To understand, one must experience, and to experience, one must explore. To step into the unknown, to tread where others dare not, that is a profound wisdom."

I went to move my pawn but Cai Lun beat me there. He took his own soldier with my piece, fxe6, and slid his priest up next to the gap at g6.

My dux!

My mind sobered for long enough to panic.

Cai Lun looked disappointed, he knew the conversation was over. "Are you a Jew, my son?"

"Yes."

"Are you really from Judea?"

I met his gaze; his eyes had not left my face for the past five moves, somehow entrancing me to lose. *How much should I let this man know about me?*

"Yes."

"That story about the boy in the street, and your lover, is all that true as well?" he asked, a tone hypnotizing me, commanding me to answer.

"…yes," I said, "…all of it." I heard my words, just above a whisper, meant for Cai Lun alone.

"You better move your dux, Jew." His hand was on my silver piece before my eyes lowered, already taking me out of check. "We never made a wager, son."

The thick fog settled over my head again but I knew he was moving in for the kill.

Cai Lun dropped a satchel of ingots on the table, spilling half of them and mixing with the lantrunculi pieces he had taken.

∞f4

Was that his priest? I could not track his moves anymore, the whole room began to blur.

"Your mother must have been a wonderful woman, and brilliant, to birth such a talented strategist," he said.

I could feel his gaze boring a hole in me, trying to steal my focus. I pushed hard on my eyes, trying to clear the murk that had set in. I could see what I had to do, but Cai Lun beat me to the piece. He took my pawn to b5, then his to a4.

That move I caught. Get my priest to b7 and I can make a move on his dux.

I felt the veil lift for a moment; I moved my priest and he returned with his castle at e1.

Perfect!

The room went dark as fast as it had cleared. My sight was gone and I knew the fear on my face was obvious. I was blind. Whatever Cai Lun had been doing to me, whatever he put in my beer, it had now taken full effect. My mind was sober now, only my sight was gone. I tried to imagine the board, knowing what was at stake.

"When I first moved to the Han," Cai Lun's voice rang out in the darkness, "a chef there taught me how to make Hong Shao Rou. Have you tried it?"

I shook my head slowly fighting to keep back the tears.

"Of course not," he continued, "Jews don't eat pork." His voice was at once soothing and condescending. He knew exactly what he was doing to me. "Hong Shao Rou takes patience, temperament, and balance. The layers of pork fat render off with the fire to reveal a black, lacquered finish, worthy of the most regal emperors."

I heard him move a piece, my piece; I recognized the sound of my marble on the wood board.

It must be my solider to d5.

Another piece moved. His this time.

Maybe his priest, he was setting it up but it sounded like he moved it back a space. g3?

"I learned a lot making Hong Shao Rou. I burned my hands more times than I can count on the sizzling pork fat. But the dish taught me to be patient."

The sound of silver, my silver. My dux one space over to c8.

"To take your time with every task," he said.

Some piece takes something, maybe at b5.

"To never lose faith in the most important thing in the world." His voice reminded me of my father talking over me while I worked in the shop.

Another piece down at the same square, b5.

"Cai Lun?" I called out, a helpless baby.

Cai Lun answered in Latin, "We are almost done, just be patient."

"I don't speak Latin," I could hear my voice tremble. My whole life was in that pile of silver I had won. I heard six more moves. I was too scared to trace them, and could only wait for the blow. A quiet clink, metal on wood teetering back and forth, brought my eyesight back. Cai Lun's finger was on my dux, playing with it. His priest had moved into position at a6; there was nothing I could do. I looked up into his eyes for mercy; when I looked back down, my dux was gone.

"Good game, son. I know you don't have the money to cover the silver, but I will take what you have. I hope it's not all of it."

It was…

"Did that go as planned?" I asked, knowing he had tricked me.

"We all fail from time to time. Maybe we can play again tomorrow night?" he answered.

I reached out my hand for the dux. Cai Lun shook his head, and that was it. I stood and turned to leave. I could feel Cai Lun's eyes on my back.

What the hell am I going to do?

Chapter 3

I turned to theft to eat, and I came to understand desperation. I knew why Mary did what she did, what she had to do. Hunger has a powerful hold over our sense of right and wrong. Living in the gutters of Seleucia showed me what it meant to be poor, desperate. I had nothing left and nowhere to go.

I spent most nights in the corners of the city market, Zarathustra. It stood alone from the rest of the city, surrounded by high granite walls to protect the riches within. Merchants sold everything from slaves to silk. The shop fronts were put up and taken down each day to keep the thieves like me from stealing at night.

The largest stand in Zarathustra also happened to be the most adorned, a fruit peddler somehow managing to secure the most ornate of decorations. I never knew the merchant's name but he was large, bald, and always wore robes of purple. His skin was weathered by the hot desert, and he carried a horsetail fly swatter to keep his fruit clean.

The stand was garnished with the same color silk as his robe and laced with gold and silver bangles at the corners. Each pillar was made of intricately carved elephant ivory, interlaced with what appeared to be rubies. Had he left any of these items up at night, they surely would have been picked clean by the scabs of Seleucia.

The day he first put his dates up at his center stand was ten days since the game with Cai Lun and ten days since I had eaten. The thought of a date was maddening. They stood there, day after day, glistening in the sun like jewels, growing riper and sweeter with each hour. My guilt from coveting those dates nearly drove me to madness.

I made Zarathustra my home just to be close to the dates. Most of the beggars and thieves joined me. The fortunate ones were able to scrape a meal together from refuse; the rest of us got by on the smell, the smell that reminded us of what food was and distracted us from hunger.

I went twenty days without food before I could find it in myself to steal a date. It is never more obvious how hungry you are until you are surrounded by those who cannot get enough. In the teachings I listened to as a child, zealots equated theft with murder. Looking back on those teachings and who spoke them, it was always merchants or those who had money that preached them hardest.

I pored over in my head what Cai Lun had said to me about

momentary ethics. I began to question the teachings so many took as truth. He was right; I had no idea who I was.

Seleucia had brought me nothing but regret. I regretted not forgiving Mary. I regretted not having the courage my father had. I regretted leaving my home and dumping my money into the hands of a trickster from the Han—despite his wise nature. I grew more comfortable with theft. Though I only stole to eat, it was strange how natural it felt.

Eventually, my quick fingers caught the attention of the Mithradates gang. Their leader, of the same name, stopped me mid-nab as I was lifting a necklace from a corner stand of a fat Zoroastrian.

I nearly throttled Mithra right there for blowing my supper for the next month.

"You have developed a talent for this, my young friend," he whispered, my hand clenched in his. "I could use another Jew in my following; they are always useful in the desert when we must barter."

At that, he placed a large helping of meat and bread in my free hand and showed me a grim smile.

Khshayarsha must have told him about me.

After six months living off of stolen food and discarded water, Mithra hired me to join his caravan across the desert into Merv. The most notorious gang in Seleucia asked *me* to join them. We set off into the wasteland with no horses or camels, only the food, water, and weapons we could carry. I wasn't sure of Mithra's intentions, but I wanted to be rid of that city.

Mithra, was a thin, agile man. He wore a head covering of knit linen, endemic to the desert nomads. He had two expressions that he would switch between with the slightest of provocations: fury and joy. There was no middle ground with Mithra; he either loved you or would gut you in your sleep. I would not say I respected the man, but I was terrified of him.

We set off from the eastern gates of the city. The sun was setting and a wide expanse of blank sand lay in front of us, an open sea of throat swelling desiccation. After eighteen months in Seleucia, I was free. No longer regretting every moment of my existence. I knew the trek to Merv was long, but my spirits lightened every day we moved away from that awful place.

Growing up and playing in the desert meant I was accustomed to the rhythm of travel on sand. We moved mostly at night, finishing our days at dawn and disembarking at sunset. We caught what sleep we could in the harsh midday sun and searched for water whenever plants were present.

I have always found desert treks the hardest. You become comrades with thirst. What little food is eaten can never be washed down properly. Urine and shit become foul, and the company...even fouler. Yet as much as I hated it, I knew it well.

Mithra typically traveled with seven bandits; I was the eighth. We didn't have much common ground, and they didn't have the patience for games. I only spoke to two of them, if I spoke at all.

Khshayarsha was there too, and as much as I hated the man, he was better than Mithra. Khshayarsha was the muscle and he knew it. I feared the man from the moment we met, but he was even-tempered enough, never lashing out at me with cause. Khshayarsha spoke to me solely to persecute; I was unsure where he was born, but he hated the Jews. Every opportunity he had, I was instructed on this.

Mithra's third in command and Khshayarsha's closest friend was Pantelies. Pan was Greek and looked it. No matter the conditions he looked like he had just docked his boat from the sea with long, golden hair and bronze, un-burnt skin. Pan's sole purpose was to please Khshayarsha. He followed the man around like a pet, cackled at every jest, even served him meals.

The two of them wearied me, but the company was an improvement over the gutters of Seleucia.

Mithra did not speak to me after that first meeting until we had been out for a week.

"Jew!" he called from behind when we were walking silently. I met him in the back for our private meeting.

"The men say you were infamous for your work at the lantrunculi table. Do you think you could make me money betting at this game?"

His confidence in me was infectious; this was the first man who had spoken to me as an equal since Cai Lun. I did not hesitate to agree. "I know I can make you, your men, and myself some money, but we need to agree on the split first."

Mithra broke into laughter. "Spoken like a true Jew! We'll discuss terms later. Right now, if you want to work with my men, you have to share the load."

He threw me his pack, considerably heavier than my own, and

sauntered up to the front of the caravan.

The trek across the open desert form Seleucia to Merv was one thousand Roman milliarium, about a twenty-day march.

Not much happened on the journey. Khshayarsha and Pan tormented me. We ate salted meat. We drank stagnant water when we could. We walked.

The entire journey stayed within the boundaries of the shrinking Parthian kingdom. As we reached the outskirts of Merv, we drew closer to the border of the newly-forming Kushan Empire. This was the first time I had heard of such a kingdom.

Mithra had traded with Kushan soldiers over the past few years and heard some of the legends.

"Ku-ju--la Kass--asa, or some shit like that," Mithra slurred, "is supposed to be the son of some general. He loves his guts and glory. He tries to be the new Alexander, Lord of Asia. All I know is Kujula is making my trade harder than it has to be."

It was near dawn and the fire was dying. It made Mithra's story that much more dramatic.

"I heard," Pan bragged, "this Kushan king fucks little boys."

"Really, Pan?" Mithra waved his hand to dispel the rumor. "A king of most of Asia, he can fuck whoever he wants, and he does it to little boys?"

"Then he guts 'em," Pan continued, trying to make the story even more impressive.

"Shut up, Pan," Khshayarsha bellowed. "You've never even heard of this guy."

At that, we stopped and tried to sleep in the increasing heat of the sun, eager for night to grant its reprieve once again.

It was after midnight, but we reached Merv in only a few hours. The city was little more than an oasis surrounded on all sides by a crude sandstone wall. The city looked as if it had been torn down and rebuilt more than twice.

The gates were built out of a stone smoother than Roman marble. The arch spanned ten pedes higher than the rest of the wall.

The caravan wasted no time. As soon as we entered, the men spread out and began peddling their stolen wares.

"Jew!" Mithra said, "I want you to take what you can from the richest marks you can find. Scout out any serious games. Double your profits over night, or at least pay me back the food I loaned you. If you do not come back with money…" He paused and cracked his knuckles.

I knew, from the onset, joining this troop meant stealing. Yet now, looking at my night's work square in the face, the reality hit me. I had become a thief.

Fearing for my life and having no desire to be hungry again, I agreed.

"What's a 'mark?'" I asked.

Breaking into his donkey laugh, Mithra grabbed me by my shirt. I could smell the reek of a month's worth of preserved meat on his breath.

"I brought you here to make money. Nothing else! You find the dumbest people you can, and you steal whatever your, tiny, dirty, Jew fingers can pull. If you do not make me an *uncial* of silver by sunrise, I'm going to cut off your hands, and I'm going take every crime tonight and lay it on your shoulders. You can take up your grievances with the Parthian guards or with the desert. Your choice."

My entire body began to shake. "Yes, sir," I said.

I had no idea how much an uncial was, but I assumed it was more than I could make stealing. My plan was to find a game of lantrunculi and steal from one man instead of dozens.

I spent hours wandering the streets of Merv, desperately trying to find a group of players. Little of the town's inhabitants could be discerned in the dark. All the people out at that hour were trying to rob each other anyway.

The moon was beginning to set when I finally found an inn, crowded with the familiar reek of drink. I peered into the candlelit room, casting a shadow over a small table surrounded by lantrunculi players. It was a relief to know I might be able to keep my hands.

Before entering, I emptied my satchel of rations and filled it with small stones. I tried to match the weight of a sack full of silver, hoping no one would look inside. The smell of drink and soiled recreants washed over me like a hot bath of self-deprecation.

"What do I owe to play?" I asked the innkeeper as gruffly as could manage.

Visibly exhausted, the innkeeper gave me a once over, his eyes landing on my satchel of stones. "If that sack is full of anything but sand, that'll do."

My heart stopped.

"Why would I carry a bag of sand? It's si—silver, from winnings in Seleucia."

He shrugged. "Papak?" the innkeeper called over to one of the players in the corner. "Are you sober enough to play?"

Papak looked up from his cup. "I play better when I'm drunk and have shit left to win. Send him over."

Clutching my satchel, I sidled through the crowd. Papak was splayed out over a recently lost game, drinking to his defeat. The table had only three legs, wobbling as I sat down. I pulled out my satchel, and dropped it on the table, careful not to let my lies spill out.

"Is this enough?"

Papak sat up. "That's certainly more than *I* have," he replied. "Black or white?"

"White," I said as I pulled the lantrunculi board and its pieces from underneath his cup. I quickly ordered my pieces, using a small hunk of wood for my dux.

Papak hadn't moved.

"Are you going to set up your pieces? I'd like to play before morning."

Papak straightened and waved a scolding finger at me. "Do *not* tell me what to do!"

He ordered his pieces in such a sloppy manner I couldn't even tell what was a pawn and what was a soldier. The dux was half in its space, half in the queen's; his castles were still outside the board. He gave the placements a cursory glance. Satisfied with his disaster of a defense, he motioned to commence.

I nodded. "We agreed you move first."

Papak was black, player two, but I wanted to test just how drunk he was.

He resigned, making his first move, throwing his queen onto a d5 space straight down.

"Does that work for you?"

I straightened his piece. It was barely in the square.

"Have you been playing all night?"

Papak looked up. "I am not fond of Jews; just fucking play."

His mood was beyond the little charm I had, so I tried to shut up, keeping my fear from spilling over.

I moved a pawn out to d4, slid it back, and then changed it to e3.

He threw his dux out right away, next to his queen at e5.

Does he want to lose? The dux can't even move that far.

Papak turned to the side and vomited on the floor, kicking up a cloud of dust. He wiped the spittle from his chin and took another drink.

I moved my soldier out to f3, realized my mistake, and quickly changed it for another pawn at f4.

Papak gave a grim smile, stole the piece with this dux, and returned to the drink.

Did he really just do that? Drunk as hell I suppose.

The dux was mine in five moves. I'm not sure if he was a fool or just too drunk to realize. I slid my pawn over his small brass piece, then reached over the table to take the purse he had sitting next to him.

He snatched my wrist as I leaned in. "We all lose sometime... Jew."

The stench on his breath shot me out of my seat. He gave me a toothless grin, and threw the purse at me. I took the brass dux as well, hoping I might trade it for a meal, and ran out.

By the time I found Mithra again, it was near sunrise. I eagerly palmed the satchel of silver I had won and handed it over to Mithra. He opened it and his face turned an impressive shade of purple.

"Jew...why are you handing me a bag of iron slag?" He held the bag open wide and dumped it in the sand. Chunks of worthless metal hunks smacked to the ground.

I had assumed I was the only one in the inn clever enough to bet with fakes. I looked up at Mithra's face, hoping for a sliver of mercy.

Without a word, Mithra grabbed me by the neck and called the rest of his men over, screaming to Khshayarsha. "Hold him here. If he moves, kill him."

Khshayarsha traded grips around my throat. I instantly wished Mithra would come back. Khshayarsha's hand was wrapped around my throat like a noose, and he delighted in my squirming. Now he knew all those fights were about to end.

Khshayarsha had spent the evening with women. Paid? Consensual? Forced? He probably didn't know the difference. But I could smell their stale cum on his breath and hands.

"I told Mithra not to bring a Jew. I told him you would do nothing but lose our money. Maybe, if you are lucky, the Kushans will take over this part of the world and you can be a pretty boy for that Ku-ju-ala."

Khshayarsha stumbled over the words, too dim to master a foreign language. "Hopefully, Pan was right. You are small." He began to pet me with his free hand, playing at our situation.

Mithra couldn't have returned fast enough. Behind him walked four guards, all carrying clubs, all perturbed to be working this early in the morning.

Mithra dropped a bag of silver at my feet. It must have been a small portion of what his men had stolen through the night. He looked me in the eye, numb and listless.

"This is the man, Kurush," he said to the captain of the guard. "This is the man who took from all those poor tradesman and prostitutes last night. Do what you want with him."

As soon as he was done, Kurush came in close.

He looked me in the eye and spat in my face.

"You think you can walk through our kingdom, take what you want, and walk back? I would like to see after what we are going to do to you. Are you ready...boy?" Kurush clubbed me and I blacked out, the odor of Khshayarsha still strong in my nostrils.

Chapter 4

I awoke chained to a cell wall with thirteen other men. Some looked as if they had been there for years. No one spoke.

The regret I had felt in Seleucia returned.

Why did I leave home? My restless nights were filled with images of Bar-Abba. I wanted to escape him, but the thoughts wouldn't leave. My mind's eye imagined the man I had never met but had been chasing me since birth. Was he my father? My place may have been with Mithra. I saw Bar-Abba as large as Khshayarsha: larger, stronger with the same stench on his breath and hands: the smell of Mary and of my mother. Thick, tufted hair full of blood. Dense, matted beard full of spittle. I awoke to Bar-Abba's hands around my throat, slowly squeezing, only to find my shackles where his hands had been.

The days drew out, slowly, one after the other, weakening me, body and spirit. The guards watered us every three days and fed us once a week, enough to keep us alive, a life no one in that cell wanted. That was the point: to live and wish only for death. No torment could have been greater. The men of Merv delighted in watching our lust for life fade until there was nothing in the cells but the husk of a man, a shadow of a living thing.

You had two choices in that prison: take your own life when you had the strength, or let a life devoid of hope drive you to madness.

Three months I spent in that cell, my grip on reality slipping.

I saw Mary, lying spread eagled in her reed lean-to. Dozens of men were lined up in the alley, lust in their eyes. One after the other, they fucked her over and over, until finally, Bar-Abba finished the job, killing her when he was done.

Cold water splashed across my face, pulling me from my haze and into the cell.

Just let me die!

"How long has this man been here?" a familiar voice asked, or maybe my mind is still murky.

"Three months or so. We picked him up for robbery. These Jew bastards always end up here."

The voice became real. It was Cai Lun. Cai Lun and Kurush.

I heard a crash of metal on the ground, a bag of silver.

"Now will you set him free?"

"Guards! Bring the keys. Release the Jew rat. We're done with him."

I hadn't stood for weeks and barely had the strength to crawl, let alone walk. The guards unclasped the shackles around my neck, ankles, and wrists and dragged me out of the room.

I could hear Cai Lun's soft footfalls as the guards took me into the open. A blast of cool air hit my face. It had been months since I had a fresh breath. Sitting right in front of the prison doors was a small, linen-covered cart pulled by two horses.

Cai Lun jumped onto one of them. "Put him in the back."

They tossed me onto a wool mattress. It enveloped me like a pleasant dream, the first in months.

I was free of that place but couldn't help but wonder why this thieving Han had taken me. What disease-ridden fantasies did he have in store for me? If I had been strong enough at the time, I would have run; as it happened, I couldn't move.

Sleep took me instantly. The last thing I heard before drifting off was Cai Lun thanking the guards and kicking the horses into motion.

What else could this man put me through? Hasn't he done enough?

I sat up with a start as the cart slammed to a stop. I could hear the horses panting loudly and Cai Lun speaking to them.

He threw open the linen tarp covering the back door, and the late sun filled the cabin.

"Good morning, friend, it is nice to see you open your eyes," he said.

"How long have I been asleep?" The words came like cold molasses. The guards had forbidden us to speak and I had almost forgotten how.

A smile streaked across his face.

"We have traveled far from Parthia. It has been three weeks since we set off."

Three weeks? The last thing I could remember was being thrown into the cart. How could that have been three weeks ago?

"Cai Lun… Why were you in Merv and why did you take me from that prison cell? What do you want with me?!"

I wanted to be angry, I wanted to hate him. He was the reason I was here, but I couldn't muster the emotion.

The smile vanished and wonder replaced it. "We will get to that later. For right now: I paid for your release as a master purchases a slave. You *are* in my debt."

I could tell the man had plans, and that his interest was sincere. Really, what choice did I have but to trust him?

I peered outside to behold the first mountains my eyes had ever seen. Golden, sheer, and impenetrable. In an instant, I saw just how small and useless I was. Tossed from cage to cage, master to master, like a mongrel pup no one wants. "Where are we?"

Cai Lun stepped back from the cart door to better my view. "This is the Pamir road. It runs from the lower areas of Bactra all the way to Kashi. Behold the newly formed Kushan kingdom."

As he spoke, a maniacal grin spread across his face. Glee was rushing through this man's veins. I could hear it in his tone, and I watched it spread over his skin like a hot burn.

Cai Lun did have plans. What did they have to do with me?

The view was beyond imagination. Cai Lun had set out from Bactra, three hundred milliarium south-east of Merv, a week prior and we were already halfway across the Pamir range.

It was summer, yet the mountains were deep in snow. I had seen frost on plants deep in the desert on cold nights, snow the road to Damascus, but never anything like this. Our cart was deep in a valley, bordered on its northern edges by the endless mountains. The peaks scratched the heavens; the tallest must have been more than a milliarium from the valley floor. The deep snowpack slowly tapered from the peaks into the rivers and streams of the valley where we stood.

Cai Lun had stopped in a field crowded with alpine brush and hardy lavender blossoms. The ceaseless mountain breeze mixed with a field of emerald was intoxicating. The acrid sap of nearby trees increased the moisture in the air. I felt so far from home yet at peace, as if I belonged in this place.

"Have you ever been into the mountains? There are not many peaks where you are from."

"No, Cai Lun, this is the farthest away from home I have ever been. I have never seen such an intense…scene. Where're we headed?"

The smile returned to my owner's face as he reached out his hand to help me out of the cart. I slowly made my way to the foot of the bed and attempted to stand. It had been months now since I had used my legs, but part of their former strength had returned. I stepped into the open field and gave Cai Lun an inquisitive look.

"Strange…I can walk. I must have been on my knees in that cell for three months?"

"More than that probably. This is why I brought you…to ask questions."

He paused, waiting for a response that didn't come.

"I aided in your recovery. Having traveled to so many parts of the world, I have learned a great deal about medicine. I will teach these things to you, but you must pay me in two ways."

"Yes?"

"First, always ask questions. Question me, question this place, question our horses if you must, but ask. Second, travel with me back to the Han and work as my assistant."

"Assistant?"

Cai Lun held out his open palms, looking into the folds of his hands. As if out of thin air, a dux from a lantrunculi set appeared. It was the dux he took from me in our last game, the dux my mom gave me as a child. My silver dux.

"How…How is this possible?"

Cai Lun held the dux up; the silver caught the light of the setting sun and reflected back into my face.

"I perform feats of wonder for my audience. That was one of many. Small but useful for taking the money from unsuspecting travelers. As is slipping a bar keeper ten silver coins to poison a beer."

What?

Cai Lun palmed the silver dux with a flash and instead handed me the sack of silver I had lost to him in the game.

Now he gives it back?

"Cai Lun, I have little need for money…now," I said, weighing the satchel. "I lost this to you. The game would mean little if the consequences didn't exist. The dux you have. My mother made that for me. I'd like that back though."

I was trying to keep calm. His admission to ruining my life was infuriating, but I didn't know what else he was capable of. I saw him drop Khshayarsha with a single kick. No telling what else Cai Lun had up his sleeve.

"You are correct. You don't need money. No man does. I simply gave this back to you because I didn't win. At least not honestly." He

42

pointed to the sack. "Look inside."

On top of my pile of winnings was my family dux. "What do you mean, you didn't win?"

"My Jewish friend, you are one of the most skilled players I have ever seen. I sat down with you that day to test *just* how skilled. I came to Merv to find you. You thought you could win amongst all those thieves without developing a reputation?"

"No one knows my name."

"Not yet," Cai Lun said. "Speaking of. You still never answered my first question. I'm *not* calling you Zeus."

I can't remember the last time someone used my actual name.

"You know what?" he interrupted. "Forget it. What's in a name anyway? I want you to know who *you* are, not what you father called you. How does Jiu Zhu sound?"

"I'm not sure. What does it mean?"

"Don't worry about it. For now, it means you," he said. "If we are heading to the Han, it's probably best you take one of their names, like I did. They can't pronounce western names anyway."

"Jiu Zhu," I tried.

"Close. Jee Choo," he corrected.

He paused to take in the mountains.

"Anyway. You do not owe me for the payment to the Merv guard. You owe me because I am offering you an opportunity to change who you are and who you could be. Hence the name." He mumbled the last part. "Going down the path, trying to figure out who you are, may take you places you do not want to be. But that is the point! You ended up in a prison in Merv for just this reason. Enough talk. Let's get a fire going. The sun will set soon. These roads are cold at night."

Cai Lun handed me a hatchet. "Go get us enough wood for the night, and drink as much water as you can."

I took stock of his humble abode before departing. His cart was full of things I did not yet understand. What I thought was linen was in fact silk. I had seen silk robes on the Roman prefects and on the merchant stands in Seleucia but never this large. The silk was inlaid with small designs, embroidered into the fabric with a master hand. It was soft to the touch but thicker than it appeared.

I walked to the front of the cart and stroked each of the horses. These horses were much larger and stockier than those used in the deserts.

They stood nearly half the height over again of a standard horse. One was a jet black and shimmered in the fading light, similar to the coat of a crow. The other was white and Cai Lun's obvious favorite, as it was well groomed and meticulously clean, considering the journey.

Cai Lun called out to me from the camp. "Do you like my horses?"

"They are fine animals," I replied. "Strong to pull two men and all those tools."

"The black is Aesop; the white is Agape. They have been with me for years. I must admit I spoil Agape. He is putting on far too much weight. Aesop gets jealous, but he works hard regardless. This breed I discovered myself."

Cai Lun joined, petting his favorite.

"Before I relocated to the Han, I went in search of a sturdy breed. I traveled as far north as Rome had conquered and then further. I sailed across a small ocean that ended in tall, pearl white cliffs. They say a warrior is only as strong as the horse that carries him. Why should I not take the time to find the perfect breed?"

Agape and Aesop whinnied under their master's touch.

"This was a land Rome had long sought to conquer but had only a few outposts at the time. Many of the inhabitants were of an old tribe, practicing rituals and traditions long believed to control the earth. As a man of rationale, this seemed unlikely but my inquisitive nature drew me on, deeper into that island.

"There, I found monoliths of solid granite. Ten times the height of a man they stood. Numerous and intricately arranged in concentric circles. The indigenous people worshiped at these sites, performed rituals."

The horses reclined on the Alpine brush.

"I spent weeks searching and found nothing. Some deer. The native tribes. A hare every now and then. But no horse to call my own. When I was heading back, a few milliaria from the white cliffs, stood Aesop and Agape. They played together as brothers. Most wild horses will run away when approached, but Aesop and Agape ran to me. These had to be the animals I was looking for. I rode them in turns back to the sea and landed back within the northern reaches of the Empire. They have been with me ever since."

I fed each horse a tuft of grass, stroking their thick manes, then set off to fetch the wood.

With each step, my legs felt stronger. I wasn't sure what Cai Lun had done but it was effective. The air seemed thinner up here, more difficult to pull into my body, but my legs felt rejuvenated.

I found a patch of knee-high pinyon pines. The effort in swinging the axe was harder than it should have been. I had to pause every few moments to catch my breath. After an hour of chopping and gathering, I was too tired to continue.

My master had made quick work of erecting a shelter. A small tent perched on the ground a few paces from the cart, the thick silken covers laid across it.

"That took longer than I expected. Do you still feel weak?" he asked.

"I'm not sure. My legs feel strong, my body feels able, but I can't seem to catch my breath." I dropped what was left of my woodpile near our shelter and stood for a moment to take in several gulps of air.

"That would be the elevation. I forgot you've never seen the mountains. We are nearly three milliaria up; those mountains to our north reach another milliaria above that. High even for me.

"Thankfully, this is as high as the road goes, and the pass skirts around the mountains, not through them."

Cai Lun stacked a portion of the wood into a neat pile, withdrawing a small metal tube from his bag along with a black stick and his knife. He shaved off a portion of the stick into the pile and struck the metal tube above it with his knife.

A shower of red-hot sparks shot into the wood. It caught fire instantly, the flames engulfing the sap-laden tinder, lighting up the camp in an inviting glow.

I was too stunned to speak. Cai Lun looked into the fire.

"You like my fire starter? The tube is made of a metal only found in the Han. The black flint you can find anywhere. My knife is the secret though. The metal tube and the metal in my knife are different; they are two opposing metals that create heat when rubbed together. When the sparks strike the wood and flint shavings, it makes fire. Effective and simple, like a tool should be."

He handed me all three items. The knife was light and sharp with a curved blade swirled with streams of white. The shine of the blade looked like water and shimmered in a similar way. I had never seen such a metal.

The artistry in the handle was as meticulous as the blade. It was carved from one uninterrupted piece of ivory, no rivets or seams. It was as if the blade and handle were one. I had carved and assembled many handle guards in my father's shop, but the craftsmanship of this blade was beyond me. The metal tube and flint were not nearly as intricate. They were tools of the open road. Function over form.

I returned the fire kit to him. "It seems you have a lot of secrets. Almost magical."

This was a man I had sorely misjudged. I had thought Mithra my savior and Cai Lun a thief. Adolescent arrogance is a dangerous character trait, one I had to subdue. Besides, I was getting a little old for such childish comparisons.

As we spoke, the sun set behind us, lighting up the valley with a brilliant pink hue that reflected off the mountain snow like a mirror. The growing fire lit up Cai Lun's face, catching only half of his features.

"Nothing I do is magic; it is something much more important and much more profound. Magic is what we call mysteries before they are unlocked. The making of fire was long held as miraculous, a gift brought down by Prometheus. The construction of my fire implements may evade your uneducated mind, but that does not make them special."

He moved in and out of the firelight, creating a dance of shadow over his face.

"When I asked you to question, this is the heart of what I meant: to unlock these mysteries. The only thing that sets a wizard apart is his questions. Wizards, witches, fortune tellers: they provide certainty in an uncertain world."

"I'm not sure I understand," I said.

Cai Lun pulled a small trinket out of his robe. It glowed opalescent in the moonlight. No larger than a coin, he began flicking it between his fingers. His hands moved faster and faster as the glowing coin began shooting in and out. Soon, I could not see it at all.

"Your religious teachings have been developed to best control your environment. Those who came before you sought answers to questions. Why are we here? What makes the sun rise, the moon shine, the mountains soar? Is man unique? Your religious doctrine represents the summation of many before you pondering these questions."

The coin shot into the air, then vanished. A log in the fire cracked loudly, sending sparks the moment the coin disappeared.

"If those that came before you had the courage to ask why, so can you, so should you."

With a smack, the coin popped into view on Cai Lun's open palm, as if it had never left.

He paused.

"I must apologize for rambling. Exile on the road does not lend itself to productive conversation. Let's eat and rest."

"I'm not sure I ever set out to find truth—but I am hungry," I said, returning to my childish amazement.

Cai Lun pulled two small birds from behind a rock. They had already been slaughtered, gutted, and plucked.

"Mountain pheasant?"

"Please."

He took the birds, skewered them, and began turning them over the open fire. From his pocket he pulled out a small, wooden box of salt and carefully seasoned our fowl.

"Salt is key, both for flavor and texture. I carry as much as I can on the road. Some pay for small quantities as well. It is a wonderful panacea. Things you care about as an ex-chef."

To me it looked like he was over-salting the meat. He picked up my worried eyes.

"Don't worry, Jiu Zhu, I was always a great cook."

"Cai Lun, you're not from the Han...are you? Why travel so far from your home?"

"Why did you?"

I really feel like he's over-salting it.

He hesitated for a moment to consider the question, a long train of thought passing through his mind. "I was born in Macedonia, once a free and mighty empire. I grew up hearing stories of Alexander and Phillip. But I knew nothing of greatness; these were legends to me. As I said, I was a baker and chef. I married when I was near your age, and had my first son a year after. My wife...Agape—" Cai Lun stopped to bury his discomfort. I saw the pain in his eyes, only for a moment, but it was there."—and my son Aesop. We owned a bakery in Pella. It was a simple life, and one that I loved. It was not uncommon for soldiers to loot local merchants, sometimes worse..."

Cai Lun paused, this time for more than a few moments. The pain was gone but the story took patience in the telling.

He took the pheasants off the fire and handed one to me. It took a lot of control not to shove the whole bird in my mouth.

"I am sorry I do not have any plates or utensils. Feel free to use my knife," he said.

He motioned over to the blade I still had sitting next to me.

"And drink as much as you can. You spent a long time in the desert and then a lot longer in that prison."

"Cai Lun, if you don't want to tell this story…"

"No, this is an important tale for both of us to hear, even if it spit out of my own mouth and back into my ear…I haven't told it in years, and the telling helps."

He took a bite and continued.

"A group of Roman soldiers entered my shop and demanded everything. My wife fought. I was in the back, preparing bread. I used to be so good at making bread. My son was with Agape. He was still a newborn, ten months."

Cai Lun gnawed on the fowl.

"I came when I heard their screaming. It was too late. One of the soldiers had already sliced my wife from chest to pelvis. A second had his boot on my son's face. There was flour everywhere. Aesop was covered in it. A dusted white angel. They wanted nothing but to humiliate. He slammed his foot down. Ten months old…The soldiers left. So did I."

It was taking all his strength to tell this story.

"Did you leave to find the men that did this to your family?" I asked.

"I struggled for years with what I should do. Take my life? Take theirs? I found something…else to live for."

His pain abated the more he spoke, as if the words were the only solace needed.

"What did you find?"

"I headed north at first, like I said. When I saw the white cliffs, I knew there was more to explore, and more for me. There was something in their vastness, their height and simple beauty."

He sighed, and the dispassionate face I later grew to love returned.

"Jiu Zhu, what happened to you?"

"How do you mean?"

"Canor, the bar man at the Babak, he told me part of your story. As much as he could catch from your drunken ramblings. Some of it I pieced together from watching you?"

"How long have you been following me?" I asked, suddenly worried I didn't want to know.

"Long time. Tell me your side of the story though. Why do *you* think you're here?"

I don't know...

It made me want to cry just thinking about it. "You were right, from the beginning. About where I'm from, about who I am. I really have no idea."

The fire was dying down, and I was glad, it helped obscure the rage on my face.

"My mom," I continued holding back tears, "she was raped... at some point. I don't think she knows who my father is. A man, a beast named Bar-Abba did it. Eighteen years later he came back and had my girlfriend. I was going to ask her to be my wife. She told me the day I left. Said she needed the money. Said Bar-Abba was willing to pay."

I threw up my hands. An empty gesture to relieve some of the boiling, impotent rage.

"What the fuck is the point of sticking around after that?" I asked. "So I left. I ran away. You, apparently, know the rest."

What little light was left on Cai Lun's face showed me he cared. His cheeks were soaked with tears.

"Let's go to bed. You still need rest."

He threw a few more logs on the fire and went to the tent. I slept well that night, better than I had since leaving home.

Chapter 5

Cai Lun was awake before me. He had already eaten, fed the horses, and broken down most of camp.

"Sleep well, Jiu Zhu?" he asked, steam pouring off his body.

"I did. These skins are warm!"

"It can get dangerous up here when the sun is gone."

"What were you doing this morning?" I asked.

Cai Lun shot a proud smile and dropped to the ground. He began a rigorous series of pushups, finishing in a full handstand.

"Training. How about you?"

We broke down what was left of camp and set out. Walking at the pace of the horses tired me, but I wanted to regain my strength.

Travel along the Pamir grew easier as we descended into Kashi. My body seemed more adept at taking in air.

Cai Lun and I passed most of our time talking. Breaks were rare. He had much to pontificate and even more to teach. He told me I was indebted to him, but he was a teacher more than anything. He was fluent in Han, Latin, Aramaic, Greek, Pahlavanik, Altbacktrish, and could understand many of the regional dialects of the Goths. He would switch between them all as if he were speaking in tongues.

One of his primary rules was "to question, you must first learn." I took pleasure in learning, particularly languages. Having already mastered Pahlavanik, the others came with relative ease.

The remainder of the road into Kashi took us another two weeks. Travel through the mountain pass of the Pamir was slow, but as we reached the outskirts of Kashi, we found a quicker pace.

We reached the western gates of the city five weeks after we had set out. Cai Lun delighted with our entrance into the city; this was once the furthest reach of the Han empire, an empire he had helped build. Though the Han was now under a would-be king that threatened to destroy everything Cai Lun had created, Kashi still stood.

To me, it looked the same as Merv. Great temples and murals of past emperors stood at the city center. At the heart of the city was a flourishing silk and spice market. Merchants and tradesmen from all over the Kushan, Sarmatia, Parthia, Satavahana, and the Han met here. This was a city built for silver. Had Mithra and his men made it this far, they surely would have made a fortune of their own.

We found Cai Lun's favorite inn, one by the name of Ziying, run by a woman of the same moniker.

"Jiu Zhu," he stopped me before going inside. "Ziying and I have known each other for a long time. Our conversation might be a little… political." He tied up our cart outside the inn and gave the horses a few handfuls of grain each. "I told you bits and pieces from my past but not much. It was rude. The Han empire is massive, and old. I worked for who used to be the ruler of this kingdom, Ruzi. A few years ago, he was overthrown. It's a long story, but a gang leader, Wang Mang, took over. I left because I wanted nothing to do with a sinking ship."

"Why are you telling me this now?" I asked.

"Don't be alarmed if Ziying and I get a little argumentative," he gave Aesop a final pat and ushered me inside.

"Oh and Jiu Zhu," he grabbed my arm and whispered in Latin. "Watch your inflection, especially in the pronouns," before switching to Han.

Ziying was the first Han woman I ever met: short and light skinned. Her hair was long, impossibly straight, and dark as coal. She wore it in a tightly woven knot on her head.

As soon as she noticed Cai Lun strolling in, Ziying's face lit up. She spoke in a bubbly Han, a language I had only just recently learned, thanks to Cai Lun.

"Cai Lun! I haven't seen you in years! Your hair grows greyer every day."

She ran fingers through his thick locks.

"Please sit, I will get tea and food." She spoke fast, much faster than Cai Lun, and with a rehearsed respect.

Cai Lun bowed to Ziying and grasped her hand.

"Thank you, Ziying. We would like a room, if you have one, and board for our horses." He withdrew his hands and motioned for me to walk forward. "This is my friend, Jiu Zhu."

"Ha!" she blurted. "I'm sorry that was rude."

Ziying bowed again.

"Such an interesting name…Do you speak Han, Jiu Zhu?"

I replied in the best accent I could, careful not to mispronounce. "I do, Ziying. My master is an excellent teacher."

"This is an educated young man, Cai Lun. How is it you found one so…attractive in the west?"

51

Cai Lun burst into laughter. "Easy, Ziying, he's young—too young even for you."

Ziying shook her head playfully.

"I see many men come through Kashi, never any as well spoken or attractive as you two." She laughed and shook her head at herself. "Okay, okay...Come. Sit. Eat and I will make your rooms." She shuffled back into the kitchen and yelled for her servants, dropping all respect in her tone.

We sat at a table in the rear of the inn. It was hewn from a single piece of cherry and stained with a supple finish.

These carpenters are good.

I had never seen a table cast from a single piece of wood. The carving would take weeks. The chairs matched the table. Sturdy and comfortable.

Ziying reappeared with a tray of food and a steaming pot of tea. She placed the spread down before us and handed each of us an identical pair of tapered, wooden sticks.

Cai Lun smirked at me. "Sorry I didn't tell you about this one. This is how people of the Han eat."

He held the sticks up at the fat ends.

"These are called *titu*. Let me show you."

Cai Lun took the titu in his right hand between his two front fingers and thumb. With deft movement, he was able to pinch food between the ends of the sticks.

The food was cut and served in a way that matched the use of the titu, small bite sized pieces bursting with flavor. There was chicken dressed in a rich, citrus sauce; white rice steamed to perfection; heaping mounds of dark, leafy vegetables with a spicy sauce to dip them in; and slices of fresh berries. The tea was dark and invigorating, smoky with a subtle sweetness.

"How have your travels been, boys? Where did you say you came from Jiu Zhu?" Ziying asked, continuing to chuckle at the name Cai Lun made up.

I managed to shovel a few mouths full of the excellent chicken before answering.

"This is good, Ziying. I'm from a Roman province in the south. I set off north along the trade routes and ended up in Merv where Cai Lun took me on."

Ziying shoveled, nodding at my every word between bites.

"I know that part of the world. Judea? Many of the better silk traders came from there." She turned to Cai Lun, inhaling more chicken. "Cai Lun, where have you been? Did you piss off the emperor? Did he get bored of your tricks?"

Cai Lun looked at Ziying and performed a simple trick, making her bowl disappear from her hand and reappear in his own.

She looked amazed, if not irritated.

"No one grows tired of my skills, Ziying. I left when Wang Mang seized the throne. He had no right. I want no part in his destruction."

Cai Lun magically returned the bowl to her.

She grabbed it tight this time and hunched over the food to protect it.

"It's interesting you come back now. They say Wang Mang has started going crazy. Kashi is so far from Chang'an. Little of the capital's inner workings reach our ears. But I heard Wang Mang believes all of the land should be owned by the palace, and that he alone knows how to redistribute it. He has also declared slavery illegal. Your old friend, Liu Xiu, has masterminded a rebellion against Wang Mang. It is only a matter of time before Liu Xiu rallies enough people to usurp the emperor."

Cai Lun took to stroking his beard.

"Liu Xiu most likely wants to restore the empire back to the rightful heirs, but I don't trust this will work either. Time will tell."

I was hesitant to jump in, even as they looked to me for my input. I feigned a slow sip of tea to give myself time to think.

"Has Wang Mang used the army to institute his rule? I'm not familiar with him, but I do know that the Romans often push their ideals on subjects with force," I asked.

Both hosts appeared surprised at my analysis. Ziying was the first to respond.

"No, Jiu Zhu, Wang Mang has paid little attention to the army. He is too weak and stupid to know how."

Cai Lun was skeptical.

"This empire has many others like it on all borders. To expand further would lead to all-out war, a war that has little effect beyond the death of soldiers and civilians. If we wish to expand, it must be through the expansion of our citizen's minds."

Even to me, Cai Lun seemed naïve.

Ziying shared my sentiment. "Cai Lun, is Wang Mang not the

reason you left in the first place?"

"I left because he took power by cunning and force. At the time I believed this would be the summation of his new empire. I may have been proven wrong."

He looked into his tea as if it spoke to him before he continued.

"I *do* approve of his ideals. Still, I am confident he will fail. The man's on the right path, just not at the right time."

Ziying nodded silently and sipped her tea before clearing our dishes and showing us to our room.

If I were to judge the Han and its people on their sleeping arrangements alone, I'd say they were a bit spoiled. Two beds set opposite each other, in a room larger than my house, were covered with silk sheets and woolen blankets. A silver washbasin sat in the corner with a pitcher of clear water. Ziying placed a candle on each of our bedsides and bowed herself out.

"Cai Lun," I said once the door closed, "I apologize if I spoke out of turn."

"My Jiu Zhu! Always with the bootlicking. I told you when we first met: your payment would be in questions. You posed an excellent one. One I had not considered. Your particular experience has molded your mind. It seems you are on a greater journey than you know."

"I'm not sure about that."

"What *did* make you leave? You asked me so I get to ask."

I sat on my bed, considering the question.

Images of Mary as well as my mother flashed through my mind. The figure of Bar-Abba tormenting them both, his unkempt beard pressing into their unwilling breasts, his hands silencing their cries against the inevitable.

Inevitable. It was inevitable, all of it. Me leaving, my mother's and my lover's rape. Men must hate. Violence and hate is all that most ever know.

I had not thought of any of this until now.

"My mother told me she was raped before her and my father had been together." I choked back a few tears. "Why would she tell me that?"

Cai Lun nodded.

I paused. A moment of clarity in my turmoil.

"I left to find a place away from Bar-Abba. Maybe kill myself, maybe kill him if I ever came back."

"Did you find what you sought in Seleucia or Merv?" Cai Lun

asked.

"No, all I found were more men like him. Men that took me in."

It weighed on me still. Who was Bar-Abba? Did it matter anymore?

Cai Lun threw off his bed sheets. He stripped to a small loin cloth, revealing a tone figure beneath.

"Why, then, did you follow me?" he asked, the darkness of the room staved off only by dim candlelight.

"Did I have a choice?"

"Really?" he asked, laughter about to spill over. "I may be strong, but I saw your hands, little Jew. They could take on the world."

He stood staring, no shame in his nudity.

"I may not have shared my true intentions with you," he said after a moment. "There is something else. There is a question I believe is on the tip of your tongue, a question that might form who you are for the rest of your life."

At this, he passed out.

"Really? Cai Lun? Cai Lun?! You are going to leave it there?"

He didn't do anything but breathe.

It seemed Cai Lun had finally figured out his plan for me. Why I was so willing to follow him was strange. It was as though he'd placed me under a spell. With his magic tricks or with his wisdom, I couldn't tell.

I fell asleep fast. I saw the courageous climb Mary had pulled off deep in the desert when we were children. I relived every moment of her struggle with the cliff. The grit of the sandstone pressing against her bare feet, the pinch of her nimble fingers in the sharp stone, the burn of her muscles as she worked her way up the face, the lion's roar she bellowed at its apex.

Chapter 6

A piercing bell woke me. Cai Lun and Ziying were standing at the foot of my bed, one holding a large bell, the other a small loaf of bread.

"Eat," Cai Lun said, "and join me outside."

As soon as I came out, Cai Lun took off down the street, sprinting fast as a hare. What else could I do but follow?

We ran.

I knew he exercised like this most mornings, but I had no idea just how intense it was. The first half hour was moderate. Cai Lun moved fast but I managed to trail. The city streets trended upward, ending in a long hill. Cai Lun did not slow despite the terrain. I met up with him when the hill was over, but only long enough to catch the dust of his feet.

Kashi was laid out in a grid, and all the roads lead into the desert. When I managed to clear the southern gate, I caught a glimpse of Cai Lun again. He was kicking up a sand dune. Before I could even reach the base, he flew back down and headed into the city again.

We ran two hours. Maybe more. Time slows when you are in such exquisite pain. Cai Lun's pace was impossible to match. I am still surprised I made it back to the inn.

Ziying was waiting for us with two buckets of water.

I plopped down in a chair near the front door and begged Ziying for a cup to drink from. Instead, she handed the buckets over to me, screaming, "On your feet," spit flying from her mouth onto my face.

The two of them led me into a back room. I held the buckets up, careful not to spill any water from them. The inn opened onto a courtyard lined with sand and punctuated with what appeared to be torture devices. I was nearly correct.

"My Jiu Zhu," Cai Lun began, "this is a Gung Fu training center. Arts like this have been practiced in Han for thousands of years. We will use them to prepare."

"Prepare for what?" It was hard to talk with the buckets pulling my arms down.

"I know you are thirsty and tired. But now, you must continue."

Cai Lun walked over and gently spotted the buckets as I struggled.

"Hold those buckets as high as you can."

"Why!?" I asked.

"To live," Cai Lun answered.

Each bucket must have weighed thirty libra.

"Now hold them there for the next hour. Ziying and I will go prepare breakfast. If you feel the need to drop the buckets, feel free to start over or give up. The choice is yours."

With that, they left.

I did what I was told. The pain was excruciating. My arms and shoulders numbed. Moments dragged past for what seemed like hours.

My sweat poured. My mouth burned with thirst. My vision blurred.

The open courtyard offered no shade from the high desert sun. My muscles shivered with exertion.

My mind turned to Bar-Abba.

I imagined his hands around Mary, around my mother, fishing fat fingers into every intimate crevasse. The hot, sour reek of flesh filled my mind. The breath of Bar-Abba washed over my face, overpowering my will, robbing my resolve. His blood red eyes pierced through the veil of pain—a waking nightmare staring me right in the face. Begging me to quit, forcing me to go on.

Just when I thought I could take no more, a huge gong resounded through the courtyard, and I fell to my knees, water sloshing around in the buckets.

"Drop them!" Cai Lun said. "But do not spill a drop. That water is yours to cherish, your pain to embrace, and the only refreshment you will see all day."

I burst out into a shriek, harnessing all the self control I had to lower the buckets without spilling them and set to drinking ravenously.

My stomach had shrunk, and rejected the water just as I had finished. The whole bucket was back in the courtyard with one heave. My muscles seized as I doubled over, and would not relax. Stuck in a fetal position on the hot courtyard. Cai Lun walked over.

"Best to drink slowly, Jiu Zhu."

He bent over and straightened my body with one movement. Forcing the muscles to relax when they couldn't do it on their own was worse than the exercise.

I let out a guttural cry as Cai Lun pulled me to my feet.

Ziying had prepared fish, rice, and a bitter, salty broth. I slowly lowered myself into a chair and looked to them for permission to eat.

Ziying bowed and handed me titu.

Cai Lun poured a glass of the broth. "Drink...slowly this time. Your muscles need salt; the broth will help more than water."

I sipped as much of the broth as I could, unable to taste it in my state.

"We will spend the next two to four weeks in Kashi. Depending on how hard you train," Cai Lun said.

"Will every day be like today?" I asked.

The two of them smiled.

"Yep," Ziying said.

"Can I ask, why do all this?"

"I told you, Jiu Zhu." Cai Lun stroked his beard again. "To live."

He sat and stared as I choked down the meal.

"More specifically, we are heading into the mountains," he continued.

"Back toward the Pamirs?" I asked.

"Not exactly..."

Our morning training session always consisted of a run led by Cai Lun. My legs grew stronger and faster with each day. I was able to pace alongside him within a week. After the run, Cai Lun prepared some tortuous method of testing my will—every day a new challenge.

Push heavy boulders up and down the streets of Kashi, crouch and jump as many times as I could with thirty libra on my back, push-ups until I threw up or passed out. They all seemed simple and silly to me, but I did feel stronger.

Evening training sessions were always the same, testing my agility, focus, and balance. The back courtyard had a series of raised, wooden platforms, some the size of lily pads, others thinner than a knife blade.

Cai Lun made me a small pack. I filled it with stones, increasing the weight gradually as I grew stronger. With time, I grew to like the exercise. The threat of falling and smacking my face was a strong incentive.

When I had fallen enough times to leave a lasting scar, Cai Lun decided to step in. He fashioned a pair of sandals that covered my entire foot. The sandals were uncomfortable at first, but they grew on me.

Cai Lun would lecture as I hopped from platform to platform.

"Gung Fu is the mastery of any skill, but also the mastery of self. Your new sandals are an improvement on typical foot wear, of my own design. They will allow you to make better contact with rock without the threat of slipping. They will also force the weight of your body onto your toes, allowing for better balance and movement. The soles of the sandal are covered in the sap of a tree from the southern Han; I searched all of Kashi to find a man who would trade it. Beneath the sap is a small, bronze step. The metal helps distribute your weight.

"You must learn to control your foot placement. Master yourself and your surroundings. One false move here, as in life, can mean disaster."

He was crouched on a small shelf above me, looking down like a reverent toad.

"I like the sandals, but the pack is ungainly," I blurted out between platforms, breathing heavily as I danced.

"That's the point! The trials that lie ahead will test *everything*. If you wanted this to be easy, you could have stayed a Jewish peasant and built more tables for the Romans. I could have stayed in Pella and made bread. Our lives have led us away from easy tasks."

"Where are we—" I fell hard and slammed my face on another platform. "—going?"

"To live, Jiu Zhu! To live. Now get up!"

I silenced myself and focused. I leapt from the platform that cut my face and landed on the thinnest of the pads with a single foot. Spinning on my toe to catch the momentum of the pack kept me in place. The wood on this pad was so thin it was nearly invisible from above; my balance had improved. This platform now felt like the hard packed earth I ran on every morning.

My skills grew, my body developed, and my conversations with Cai Lun explored the inner workings of my mind. We spent four weeks in Kashi, training day and night, rarely resting. When Cai Lun finally found the missing piece we needed for our gear cache, he decided my body was ready.

Ziying filled our sacks and our cart.

"Come back to Kashi when you have a chance, Cai Lun," she said as we rode away. "If you do manage to retake the throne, remember your old friend Ziying fondly. I don't want to spend my entire life out here! Good luck." She bowed one last time.

The road south of Kashi led into Puli, the southernmost outpost of the Han empire. The trip was long, but easy. Three weeks and we were there. Cai Lun and I continued our training on route, asking me to run behind the cart with the full load of my pack. My body was in such good shape by then, I didn't even mind.

Puli lay under the shadow of a mountain chain even more daunting than that of the Pamir, a behemoth of snow and rock leering down on us, a waiting tiger.

Cai Lun pulled the cart over when the mountains came into full view and I caught up with my pack. He unhitched Aesop and let him walk free for a few moments.

"Before you, the Paropamisadae rises up like a gift, a mountain range unlike any on earth. Beyond them, the Kalakunlun. The zenith of this great chain lays five milliaria above the sea, scratching the cellar door of heaven."

I tried to stand tall and take in the view but was too winded.

Cai Lun forced Aesop into a fanciful canter. He was proud of these mountains, as if they belonged to him.

"Deep in that chain is where we are headed: to a wall of granite, seen by few men, conquered by none."

Aesop paused, out of fear or disobedience, but it added occasion to the speech. We were taken aback.

"When I set off from the western Empire, after finding Aesop and Agape," Cai Lun continued, "I moved east into the Han--not by compulsion, but by design. It has been my life goal to never find comfort. Comfort is a state of stagnation and, in stagnation, no life sprouts, only sickness."

He set the cart back in motion, kicking the horses into a full gallop.

"Come on, Jiu Zhu, keep running, we aren't there yet," he called back.

We continued south along the mountain road into Goktas. Two more weeks.

Goktas was a city unlike any other. It was a center of learning and the hub for Buddhism. We needed an inn. I needed the rest, as did the horses. But such comforts did not exist in a city of ascetics. We decided to make camp outside the gates in a small pine grove under the impressive eastern flank of the Paropamisadae. The mountains rose up, sheer as temple walls, drenched in bright white snow even as our campsite was green with the spring thaw. The trees surrounding the city were tall, thin,

60

and full of sticky sap. They smelled like desert plants and were covered in sharp needles.

When we finished making camp, we walked into the city.

"What do you know of the Buddhists?"

I shook my head. "Nothing."

"Well I suppose we will have to change that. Now pay attention." He took off in front of me, eager to get where we were going.

As we walked deeper into the city, the moon grew stronger. The streets were lined with devout followers on the path of abstinence. Some were as stationary as the statues of their idol, having collected nearly as much dust and equally uncared for. Others were stark nude, rejecting the concept of adornment. Though the ideals of this city sparked my interest, they seemed impossible to follow long term.

We headed toward a temple in the center of the city. Goktas was small but impressive, hewn from the rock of the mountains above. It was spring, but the air was frigid. The streets grew heavier with devout followers as we pressed closer to the center. All were seated in a cross-legged fashion, deep in mediation, half robed, and emaciated. I marveled at their self-control. Cai Lun and I wore our sealskin parkas. These disciples were clad only in thin linen, half of their torsos exposed.

How can they stand these temperatures and remain so still?

"The body can withstand a great many pains if the mind allows it," Cai Lun said, noticing my disbelief.

"But how do they survive?"

"Their minds," he replied.

"Is that possible? Can the mind control the body?"

"If they are one. A great many things are possible with practice."

Unlike many temples of the west, this one had no name, marked only by a rough figure of the Buddha above the entrance.

The carving was not lavish. It was of a man sitting, hands raised at heart's center, eyes closed, his face serene. The temple was an open courtyard, bathed in moonlight, filled with pilgrims. No altar, no chimes, nothing but prayer.

Most sat in identical fashion, lined against the walls; others were immersed in discussion. At the center sat an armor-clad warrior, separate from the rest. It was obvious he was not of their world. A king or perhaps a priest was my first notion. Nearly both...Cai Lun stopped at the main temple gate.

"Jiu Zhu, before we continue: What was it that made you ask about Wang Mang's negligence of force?"

"When we were discussing the Han at Ziying's?"

He nodded.

"The question seemed apt," I answered.

"That's true; it was a more astute query than you know," he retorted, lowering his voice as to not disrupt those in meditation. "Consider this. The earthly struggles of the Buddha formed the all important question: how to end suffering. That which the Buddha suffered led him to this. What do you seek?"

Cai Lun pulled me over the threshold into the courtyard.

There was little room to sit and join the other pilgrims, so I sat next to the warrior.

His military uniform was comprised of hundreds of interwoven, golden scales, completely covering his torso and legs. At his side lay a small sword, simple and functional. His helmet matched his armor, and sat at his left.

Taking my place at his side, the warrior slowly turned his head and nodded in approval. Cai Lun remained at the perimeter of the courtyard, tightly packed between pilgrims.

Those who chattered stopped when I sat next to the warrior.

The space was silent, no sound but the breathing of hundreds of men. Time in that temple was slow, my mind stayed blank. When moon light began to stream down my face, the warrior rose and walked out, pausing at the entrance. I looked over to Cai Lun who motioned for me to follow.

The man sheathed his sword and placed his helmet beneath his arm. He bowed then began speaking in Altbaktrish.

"I saw you and the man dressed as a Han priest enter together. Neither of you are citizens?"

"We are pilgrims," I replied, slowly forming each word, careful not to offend with my weak Altbaktrish. "We seek passage into the mountains to the east, and we seek knowledge of the Buddha."

"Do you seek the eightfold path?" he asked.

I assumed this was the way into the mountains. "Yes, we seek the eightfold path. What do you seek?"

"Do you know who I am?" he asked, surprised I was so open.

"I do not. I...I am just a visitor. I'm sorry."

"Don't apologize. We are strangers, you and I. Will you join me in the fields?"

With a nod I walked with him through the pale blue streets and into a lush open field.

The moon filled the sky—bright, clear, and large as the sun. We reached a small hill at the center where the warrior removed his sword and helmet again. He placed them at his side. As if selecting the most important of objects imaginable, he rummaged through the smooth stones at our feet. When he found one that suited his purpose, he continued.

"Please, sit. I wish to know your name. Where are you from?"

The moon lit his face enough for me to see a long, woven beard. His skin was dark and worn. His eyes told me his age was close to my own but deep wrinkles were set in his brow like that of an older man.

I continued carefully, measuring each phrase. "I am from the west, south of Rome. My master, Cai Lun, brought me here."

"And your name?" he asked, masking his impatience.

Cai Lun's hypocorism, whatever it meant, seemed fitting enough. "Jiu Zhu."

"I can see that you are not from the Han, so I can assume you are slave to this Cai Lun?"

"I owe him my allegiance but not my freedom. I serve him by choice. What do they call you?"

He paused, considering his own moniker as much as I had. The wind abated slightly, slowing the passing clouds over head and opening direct moonlight onto his face.

"I am called Kujula Kasasa."

My heart stopped. I remembered the name from Mithra's stories.

"Worry not, Jiu Zhu. I am here as a pilgrim, a disciple of the eightfold path, as you are. We are equals in the eyes of the Buddha. You were brave to sit next to me though."

"Please, forgive me." I kowtowed as deeply as I could, hoping Mithra's stories were false.

"Stop! Please. Rise." His voice was soft and devoid of the malice I had been warned of, yet he was clearly perturbed by my sudden change to timidity.

"Liege, I had been told—" I said to the dirt.

"Kujula, not king. Call me by my chosen name. You have been

told what? Stories?"

"Yes." My face was still buried in the earth.

He placed his hand on my shoulder. "Please stop, Jiu Zhu."

I rose and uncomfortably sat across from him.

With practiced ease, Kujula took the smooth stone he had selected and began running it over his exposed blade. The typical sound of sharpening metal was absent; it was closer to the sound of a metal on wood. This warrior knew how to care for his instruments.

"I assume you traveled through Parthia and parts of the Han. I must confess, my military campaigns have been empty of negotiation. I can understand why those men hate me. But I assure you, I am a servant of the people. I expand our empire to keep other kings from doing the same to us. I want room for my people, not a kingdom won through subjugation."

"Again, I am sorry, Kujuala. It's hard to sort out truth from rumor."

"And please. Do not kowtow to me in this place. The Buddha asks that we bow to all men as equals. In my mind that means we bow to no man. Don't you agree?"

It was clear he was trying to lure me into discussion. Perhaps he had traveled through these lands, feared for his might, and hungered for conversation. In a stranger, he might find the comradeship he sought. I obliged.

I tried to mirror his posture to put him at ease.

He instead shifted his position, slowed his honing, and pulled a small dagger from beneath his armor.

"Would you mind assisting me?" he asked.

Strange that a man so clearly concerned with the quality of his edge would trust a complete stranger. The only edge I had ever sharpened was the lathe in my father's shop.

The two of us sat in the waxing moon, focused as surgeons, honing blades. It was a quarter of an hour before I felt confident enough to continue the conversation.

"I have been subjugated my entire life. The rule of the Romans on my land is harsh and cruel. We are taught to bow from a young age; the alternative is to cower."

"The rule of Rome is legend," he agreed. "She has spread far by force. This is not something I am interested in—for myself or my people."

"Noble sentiment, Kujula. Have you heard news of the emperor, Wang Mang?"

He stumbled with his blade, sending a grating scrape through the field.

"I have. My armies push into parts of his kingdom as we speak. I am not sure his rule will last. What do you know of this man?"

"A little. I spent weeks in Kashi. News travels."

"What have you heard?" Kujula asked, thirsty for news.

"Wang Mang usurped the old grand emperor. He wants a kingdom of equality, devoid of slavery, free of land ownership."

"Progressive ideals from such an inexperienced king. He allows the armies of the Han to disband. In these times, how can we expect to instill our rules without at least the threat of force? How can we maintain our lands without their protection?" Kujula asked.

He had continued his delicate, rhythmic pace with the blade as he spoke; it had to be close to finished.

"I am no great ruler, Kujula. It seems to me that Wang Mang's hopes mirror your own."

His eyes narrowed, and his honing intensified. Sparks lit up the sparsely lit field, partially revealing features I hadn't noticed.

"I agree. I do have the same wish for my people. Though if I were to take land ownership, uprisings, I fear, would follow. Wang Mang will soon fall, either by my armies or Liu Xiu's"

The blade rang with each stroke, a bell singing in the night.

"Wang Mang's fate, it seems, is sealed," I continued. "His intentions may be for the good of the people of the Han, but I don't imagine they are ready for such radical change. Strange that good intentions are met with blinding hate."

"Tell me Jiu Zhu, why are you here?"

Staring down at my own blade; it became irrevocably obvious that this question might be beyond me. I handed the dagger to Kujula, considering it complete.

"My master and I seek the eightfold path into the mountains."

Kujula broke into laughter and did not remove the blade from my hand.

"You are still learning our language, yes? Jiu Zhu, the eightfold path is not a road; it is a way of life, the ideals of the Buddha to gain the

65

middle way. "

I guess the knife was not up to his grade of surgical precision.

Without even feeling the edge he could tell it was not yet ready.

"We also seek passage into the mountains," I answered.

"What path?" he asked. "The Paropamisadae are impassable. I do not see how these mountains pertain to anything meaningful on earth. Maybe leaving it for good."

After one last pass of his honing stone, he rose triumphantly, threw the stone into the air, and cleaved it in two as it fell.

"Wow, good work," I said. "To be honest Kujula, neither do I. This is the plan of my master."

We both laughed at the absurdity of the idea. He re-sheathed his sword, and then accepted the knife without hesitation.

"You are a trusting man, Jiu Zhu, to follow a man into immediate perils, to trust that his judgment will lead you to anything other than death. I suppose I ask the same of my men in battle... I have not spoken to a man like you in a long time. Thank you for being honest and open with me."

He paused and considered his next thought.

"If you are in Kushan again, please come to the city of Begram. You are welcome in my house. And I won't forget the name. Such a silly name for a westerner. Your master has a sense of humor."

I still didn't get it. My Han is not that bad.

Kujula wanted an empire of peace, to develop relations with the other kingdoms and open trade and commerce throughout the world. His search for the eightfold path permeated throughout his military might. It took me years to understand his ethos, but our first meeting left a lasting impression.

The sun rose, crowning the snowcapped peaks to our east and filling the lush field with life. Kujula stood with the sunrise and left.

I walked back to camp to find Cai Lun preparing breakfast.

"Did you speak with the king?" he asked, eager to hear about my evening.

"You knew it was Kujula?" I grabbed the quail he was roasting, pulling chunks of meat off for both of us.

"I did. I have not met the man, but I have seen his face on the coins of Kushan. Was he the monster of rumor?" Cai Lun asked as he cooled the hot quail.

"Far from it. A sleeping ferocity, maybe. Not very different from yours I suspect." I was famished but ate contemplatively; the conversation with Kujula had left a sense of foreboding.

Cai Lun nodded as he chomped on the sour mountain fowl.

"He talks about of the Han, Rome, Parthia, and Sarmatia as if they could unite under a single banner. This kind of world is impossible, but only because men won't allow it. It brought an idea to mind," I said, absent mindedly chewing.

I had barely finished a single leg before Cai Lun prepared another for the fire.

"Please, continue," he said.

"Kujula is as skeptical about Wang Mang's negligence of force as Ziying was. Though he is a proponent of peace, he thinks peace can only be kept through the threat of violent action—"

Cai Lun rummaged through his sack and pulled out a slab of salted fish, impatient for the quail to finish.

"You wonder," he interrupted, "why the world, why people, must be ruled through violence."

"Yes. My home is ripe with blood and subjugation. We want freedom from Rome, but the zealots wish to match arms with force. It's impossible. There can be no freedom from the Empire. Why do men feed the never ending cycle of violence? And not simply make an empire of their own lives?"

Cai Lun dropped the fish and clapped. "Very good. And that is where Jiu Zhu comes from," he said between loud applause.

"I still don't get it Cai Lun. That is not a word I've heard you or any other native Han speaker use before or since. Care to enlighten me?"

He smiled and picked the fish back up. "Some day, when you earn it."

My appetite returned. Finally being able to express my idea was cathartic, but Cai Lun's intentional enigma was still irritating, enough so that I wanted to distract myself with food.

Cai Lun smiled even more, trying to hide his laughter. It did not distract him from his feast though. He tore of a large chunk of salted fish and handed it to me.

"These are violent times," he began with a full mouth. "Lines on the map are shifting; empires are rising and falling. It would take but a spark to ignite the entire world, though I have not lost hope that it may end in peace."

He took a breath and swallowed hard. "Who will create that spark? Wang Mang may be the visionary to lead us. So may Kujula. Many others are in line to do the same."

"Cai Lun," I said, shifting our conversation. "Why are we here? I have trusted you this far without complaint. But what are we doing near these mountains?" I finished the helping of fish and went to the cart to get our water bladders.

Cai Lun looked into my face, his piercing green eyes lighting my soul again, searching for something deeper within me.

"Little Jiu Zhu, in order to lead, you must first find the leader. We need to find a spark that will not burn out. Someone who will go beyond the limits of others, find strength none knew existed, and courage none can match. I believe this man can be you. And I believe he is in the Paropamisadae. Go find him."

Chapter 7

We spent weeks in Goktas, preparing our minds and our bodies. Our training routine continued, but our days were filled with quiet contemplation. I learned much of myself while there. It came to me that those in Goktas were not so concerned with right action, as much as compassion. It was a radical philosophy, and seemed at odds with the rest of the world.

It was another month before Cai Lun spoke of the mountains again. He took me deep into the outskirts of the forest that surrounded the city. A lake nearby was fed by an incredibly turbulent river. Directly overhead lay the gates to the Paropamisadae. From the folds of his coat he took out the tool he had worked on since Kashi.

"Jiu Zhu," he called me in. I sat at his feet. "Men suffer; there is no escaping this fact." He took the tool and spun it delicately in his hands, just as he had the coin our first night in the Pamirs. "This is the Great River, remember it well. Now, why did you leave your home? What really pushed you out?" he asked.

He threw the hunk of metal straight into the air, and just like the coin, it disappeared and reappeared with a loud pop in my hand.

I sat staring at the mysterious device, pondering his question.

"When I was a child, I went into the center of Galilee to hear a zealot speak. This man, Judas, had grown infamous for his hatred of Rome's rule. He called for Jews to rise up."

I palmed the round, metal disc and found a catch on its top half. Flipping it open revealed a glass cased inner chamber. A small red needle sat at the center, suspended in water.

As I spoke, the small needle in the center began to spin, as if reacting to my inner turmoil.

"That day, his sermon came in the guise of a Talmudic lecture. The gathering hung on his every word. It took but a spark, as you say, for the soldiers to start the suffering. There was an older man holding a newborn. This man had committed no crime, hadn't raised a fist to anyone. He was one of the last ones killed by the Romans that day. The babe rolled from his hands into the street, its face was smeared with the blood of the others the Roman's killed."

I fiddled with the small metal container, trying to divine its purpose. As I turned it, the needle resisted movement, always pointing up.

"I could see the babe's eyes. It looked up into the face of a Roman, crying for help. Of course he didn't."

Cai Lun was still. If there was any emotion, he did not let it surface.

"I was just a boy, but I should have helped. I did nothing. I watched it happen, useless. I do not blame the soldiers for what they did. These men were caught up in a system of violence. When I finally learned of the man that had raped my mother, and my lover years later, all I saw were the eyes of that babe. How helpless it was to the violence around him."

I stood, turning my body to face in the same direction as the needle. It pointed me directly at the gateway to the mountains, beckoned me on.

"Can the violence of men ever be quelled? I wondered as my mother wept, reliving her rape. I wondered the same as I spoke to Kujula. Even as I mediated in these fields, the question remained."

Cai Lun nodded his head in approval, finally showing signs of life.

"You are ready, Jiu Zhu. In your hand you hold a compass. This device will show you through the mountains."

He jumped out of his seat and peered over my shoulder to ensure I was looking at the compass correctly.

"The needle will always point to the north. It is far more accurate than the movement of the sun, and when you are in the mountains, the sun's position will be strange, seeming shorter on its daily arc. Do you understand?"

"Yes, but what direction should we take through the mountains?"

"There is a place you must seek... alone," Cai Lun answered. "Tomorrow, at sunrise, you leave."

He walked back to camp. We didn't speak again the rest of the day.

And I did not sleep that night. When Cai Lun told me to find myself in the mountains, I assumed he meant with his help. I dreaded the inevitable sunrise. I wished for eternal night beneath a bank of stars. I watched the full wax and wane of the moon, the weight of my impending task crushing me, like an ocean of snow, settling in on top of my chest.

The morning came, as it always does. I was out of bed preparing breakfast before Cai Lun for the first time since we met.

70

"I take it you didn't sleep?" he asked when he saw I was up.

"No. No, I did not."

"Are you mad at me?" he asked.

"Just terrified," I answered.

"Scared is good; that means you care."

We ate in silence, a rare event in our friendship. I did what I could to muster my courage, searching for the strength I knew wasn't there.

When we finished, Cai Lun pulled a small parchment from his robe.

"I have prepared this map for you," he said, handing the paper over. "When using the compass, you will be able to navigate the mountains with relative ease. Head back to the Great River we stood at yesterday. Follow it northwest. You will be next to the river for most of the approach; your path will be marked by its coursing current, making water and food abundant. Trace the river for two days, forty milliaria or so, until it turns east."

Cai Lun traced his finger over the route he had meticulously drawn. I knew he had taken time and care to indicate obstacles and land marks. He wanted to challenge me like a father pushes a son without killing me in the process.

"There are many peaks deep in mountains. You are looking for only one to climb."

"Climb?" I stopped him.

He ignored and continued his briefing.

"Follow the torrent as it moves out from the depths of the mountains. After another two days, the waters will begin to slow and freeze. Glaciers will spill into the valley from the north. Find them on the map. The third glacier you encounter to your north marks your final approach. It flows in from a steep valley."

"But...Cai Lun? I do not know how to climb," I said.

"Really?" Cai Lun answered. "What do you think we have been training for all these months?"

He batted the map hard and continued.

"Camp at the mouth of this valley and proceed before dawn. From there, the tower is less than two hours march, three at most. As you move across the glacier, granite will open up to your east, peaks always above you. Your climb will be obvious at that point: a pillar of stone, five stadium in height, unmatched in beauty."

He hadn't mentioned the name yet, but now here it was clear on the map: the nameless tower. The beast had a name.

"Five stadium? Cai Lun, that's insane. There is no way—"

"No way to what? Do something incredible? Do you want to go back to that prison in Merv? That was quite the mediocre feat."

This whole situation seemed cavalier at best, but Cai Lun kept snapping every time I showed a hint of weakness.

He returned to his dispassionate briefing. "The face you must climb will be the first face you encounter when you approach the tower. It looks west. If you study the tower when you get there, you will see it is marred by deep cracks and groves. Every enemy has weak spots and these fissures are the nameless tower's soft underbelly."

His face went from disconnected to concerned, fatherly.

"Little Jiu Zhu, I know you are terrified. I would be worried if you weren't."

He folded the map and tucked it into my coat. The memory of my father helping me get ready for work flooded my mind.

"The nameless tower shouldn't take more than two days if you climb with little rest. By the first night there will be a large, flat, snow-filled table you can sleep on, two stadium from the base. After this first break, you won't be able to stop until you are done."

He paused, dread in his face. I began packing to fill the awkward silence. He came over and joined, gingerly laying out every piece of gear and closely inspecting it.

"When you have reached the summit, the descent will be worse. The path you took up may be your best option, though skirting the southwestern flank may also work. If you are lost in these mountains, you will die. If you run out of food, you will die. If you forget about your coat, you will die. One false step, as in life, will end in death."

I knew he was trying to create a sense of occasion, but the curt nature he metered out my life with made me drop my pack.

"Is that supposed to make me feel empowered or just small?" I asked.

"You must fight for your life every second you have of it," he answered. "You have enough food to last a month. I also made seal skin layers for your boots; these will keep your feet warm. I stitched gloves as well."

He picked up my bag and gently put it on my back, as if to say I had no other choice.

72

"Drink as much as you can during the day, but do not eat snow at night. You will be exhausted and sweaty the whole time; allow the sweat to dry before nightfall and eat right before you go to sleep."

He adjusted the belt on my bag to ensure a proper fit, and bent down to inspect the laces on my boots.

"The air is going to get thin. Every step, every movement, will require enormous effort and focus. Minor injuries will become big ones. If your weakness overtakes you and you give in to the mountain..."

He finally looked upset after all this.

"You must find a driving force to push on."

"I know Cai Lun, but I have never..."

"The tower you seek has no name. I figured the one I gave it was good enough." He stood up from my boots, holding back a mist in his eyes. "Few men have ever seen it."

He took to straightening odds and ends on my jacket and pack.

"In order to lead, you must finish what you don't even want to start. When you first see the nameless tower, every part of you will say, 'run.' When you look to shepherd men's will, you will often look down the edge of a sword. To find the man you seek, you must go where you dare not, where death is at every turn. Only faith in yourself will carry you through. They say god is in the mountains. You must find him and have the strength to peer into his face."

He gave me a hug, and walked back to our tent without turning around.

I set off from camp, no idea where to go next.

Chapter 8

The Great River surged before me. Even after two days of hiking, the torrent was deafening. The seal skin linings of my boots and coat kept me warm and dry, even in the deep waters when there was no other way to follow the river but to cross it.

Those first two days were uneventful. Travel along the valley felt like I was back in the Pamirs. The air was thin, but I had acclimated to it. I marched on an empty stomach, saving rations for what waited ahead. But I drank as often as I could, filling my stomach whenever hunger pains resurged.

I arrived at the east bend in the river before sunset on the second day, relieved I was making progress as Cai Lun had described it.

The path east was more difficult. The valley narrowed, rock turned to ice, and ancient glaciers opened up, slowing my progress. I had never negotiated such terrain, never even dreamt of it.

I reached the third and final glacier four days after the bend in the river, long after sunset, a week into my lonesome journey. I found a small cave at the mouth of the glacier to shelter in for a few hours. The moon was at its apex. The entire valley soaked up its light. The beauty around me was at once majestic and terrifying. To feel so small and so alone amidst so many dangers could humble a lion, even a king.

I did not sleep, despite my exhaustion. I kept turning Cai Lun's speech over in my head. I knew this was a man who would reject the traditions of the past; believing a deity was hidden in these mountains was not in his character.

My thoughts again turned to Bar-Abba. His haunting image pressed me forward. Why was I out here, huddled in a tiny cave, slowly freezing? Did Bar-Abba's actions force me into this place? Was he pulling the strings all along? I couldn't help but wonder as I shivered violently to keep warm. Had I come to the Paropamisadae to die?

I set out from the cave before the moon began to set.

The final approach to the nameless tower was short but strenuous. The granite walls now prevented any escape east or west; I was hemmed in on all sides. The mountains looked down on me from thousands of pedes up, judging, waiting for any misstep to send me to my death. They suffered my passage only because I refused to turn back. Yet I struggled to stare them in the face, their power over life and death loomed above me.

74

Then the nameless tower sprang up to the northeast, a lighter shade of red than the other faces, separated from them like a giant tooth biting into the sky.

Cai Lun was right: I recognized it immediately. My first thought? *This, I want to climb.*

The nameless tower did not loom over me, it offered no offense to my trespass. In fact, the opposite, it beckoned me on. I could hear it call my name.

I traced the line of the fissures Cai Lun mentioned and imagined my progress up the face. The first day's climb seemed simple enough, low in angle compared to the rest. The high table he talked about was obvious, burdened with heavy snow but flat. The goal for day one.

The final stretch of granite from the table was infinite and blank. There would be no pause in climbing, no reprieve after that first night. Though this made the climb fairly simple, it afforded me only two options: climb flawlessly or fall to my death.

The approach to the base of the tower was only a few stadiums in length, but it looked more dangerous than anything I had hiked thus far. The couloir was steep, full of talus and glacial snow pack. It looked like the nameless tower had slowly shed its skin over thousands of years.

As I stood there, estimating my travel up the pass, a shower of ice fell from the summit above, crashing into the silent valley. The gravity of my endeavor dawned on me. Everything I had hiked was on a trail. Cai Lun had drawn it all out and made sure the route was punctuated by obvious landmarks. I may have been far away from everyone and everything I knew, but there was always some life, some company. I saw birds, fish, and trees for days and I never felt alone. Now there was no life but my own. Now there was nothing but the nameless tower.

Staring down the face of the work to come, I desperately yearned for the piercing squeal of a pika, or a stoic stare from a marmot. The only company from here on would be rock, wind, and fear.

Every step was on loose rock or shifting snow. I found myself digging my boots as deep into the snowpack as I could, the snow compressing and leveling out with a kick step, the only effective method I found of forcing my way through the drifts.

The effort soaked my garments with sweat and burned my legs. I heard my heart pumping in my ears. Acid coursed through my veins.

Drawing breath was an endless effort the higher I climbed. I had to press on. Reaching the base of the tower was just the beginning. After three hours I was at the base, soaked and exhausted but ready. Taking a moment to consider my progress I disrobed to allow the newly risen sun to dry my sweat. I looked up and saw no sky, only rock, an immeasurable river of pink stone flowing upward, waiting, drawing me onward. The tower was forever above me. I removed the seal skin from my boots, drew the laces as tight as I could, filled my stomach with snow melt, and closed my eyes.

The first two stadium lengths were capped by a pair of cascading roofs. Roofs I would have to scramble over like a spider on a ceiling, like Mary in the desert. The dark rock of the roofs tapered into a section of greyer, less featured granite, creating a beautiful open book feature: my first stop on my journey upward.

The top of the roofs blanked out in a shallower section of dark granite, partially covered by snow. My initial plan was to tackle the roofs by the corner, and summit over the ledge onto the snow-filled section, traversing right onto the flat surface I would call my camp.

I found a climbing technique quickly enough, one that came naturally. Hand and foot holds can always be found on the surface of a climb—pulling up is as straightforward as using a ladder. Foot work comes just as naturally after a bit of training—the smallest of rocky protrusions feel like immense steps to those who find them. Weeks on Cai Lun's platform torture device all made sense. I was thankful for the scars it had given me.

The first hundred pedes were easy climbing; my boots found ledges as large as the wooden platforms I trained on, and I smeared the soles on the rock when there was nothing else. It was tiring work, pulling my weight over and over, but I moved quickly.

Rock fissures I found even easier and meditative. Placing my hands and expanding them to fists allowed the entire weight of my body to lock into the cracks. The crack system began near the base and leaned right as I progressed, thinning as I reached the open book.

Up to that point, the movement up the face was rhythmic. Now that the cracks were too thin to use, the climb was a puzzle, requiring precise route planning and problem solving to continue. Technique had transitioned into planning, movement, and balance.

My only hope was that my training would suffice.

I pulled over the open book and moved out onto the granite slab, finding only a few handholds large enough for the pads of my fingers.

I looked down and then back up. Two-hundred pedes from the ground, far too many still to climb. All I could see was the hemmed-in valley filled with talus. Nothing but granite in every direction. I kept moving upward. Terrified and alone, I moved upward. From the end of the crack system into the corner was only a few dozen pedes, but it took all I had to solve. My arms began to burn. My calves cramped.

When ledges were too small for my boots, I could smear them to the rock like tree sap to a newly cut branch. I grew more confident in my footwork the higher I climbed and the meditative focus on something I could control was the only thing keeping me moving. Keeping the fear at bay. Reaching the corner system was a reprieve. I moved through the next hundred pedes with ease: jamming my feet and arms as deep into the widening fissure as I could. After a few minutes, the fissure widened so that my entire body could squeeze in. I wriggled in-between the rock, and paused to catch my breath, finding comfort in the embrace.

Suspended, bridging my body between holds, encased on all sides by granite, this was a move I was most comfortable with. By forcing my weight in opposite directions on the walls, I could rest for as long as I wanted or, almost as easily, worm my way up the fissure with little threat of falling.

I pushed upward, relaxing one arm and pushing down hard with my legs. The chimney system ended in a final hundred pedes of low angled, slick rock. I easily traversed right onto the snowfield.

The newly fallen snow was thinner and looser than I had expected. I slowly sidled across, kick-stepping with my heel, traversing toward camp, toward safety.

The snow began to slip. No sound of warning. Just a slow movement toward the edge. I slid with the snow shelf, falling back toward the cliff I just climbed. The world was silent but my heartbeat was loud enough for the entire valley to hear. The snowfield began to pick up its momentum as we both tumbled toward the edge.

Running was the only option. I sprinted against the sliding snow, my feet slipping out from under me with every step. If I fell, I was done. A hand's width from the granite wall, from camp, the entire snowfield collapsed, swallowing me into the empty void.

As suddenly as it had begun, the snow stopped. Sunk waist deep, like standing idle in sand as the tide washes your feet, I found a ledge of granite beneath me, somehow stopping the snow before it careened down into the valley.

I carefully dug myself back onto the surface and delicately made my way to the rock face, only a step away. Serenity and surety at last.

The sun was setting. Twelve hours since I set out from the valley, yet it seemed like no time had passed at all.

I found a small, dry alcove protected from icefall overhead and shielded from the wind. There was a small patch of snow in the alcove. I packed as much as I could into my mouth, cooling and replenishing my sweat.

Looking out across the valley I ate solid food for the first time in days, soaking in the breathtaking desolation thousands of pedes below. It was a meager meal but the greatest ambience in the world.

A massive glacier in the valley reached deeper into the Paropamisadae, terminating at a peak to my east. Beyond that lay the great plains and the southernmost tip of the Han empire. To my northeast loomed a peak far taller than the nameless tower, reaching up another milliarium, Kechu. Cai Lun had marked it on the map. It was wreathed in cloud, birthing its own weather.

How long would these mountains endure my passage? What other surprises would they muster for me?

The sun set on the lifeless land, bereft of the influence of man, beaming with an ancient beauty.

Chapter 9

My food choices were slim. Dried salted fish or drier salted elk. Neither seemed to whet my appetite, but pulling my coat tight around me was comforting. Loosening my boots and placing the sealskin back in soothed my aching feet.

I slept that night despite the cold, and wandered into dreams.

I saw the face of Kujula, standing at the head of his great army, surrounded on all sides: the men of the Han to the north, the allied armies of Parthia and Sarmatia to the west, the glory of Roman warships to his south, and an unknown tribe standing above them all.

I flew over this oncoming battle, watching the men's terrified faces.

I landed on the edge of a cliff next to the general of the unknown tribe. He was dressed strangely, bearded and taller than most. My eyes slowly focused on his face, alien yet familiar. It was the face of the man who haunted me. Bar-Abba. It was a face devoid of fear, only determination.

His eyes turned, striking a gaze of patient revulsion. His hands shot to my neck and squeezed—

I snapped awake, eyes frozen shut. The night had brought a freezing rain and colder wind. I drew my hood over my face and held open palms to my eyes trying to thaw them.

The moon was high when my eyes warmed enough to peel them open. I decided to move on. It was cold and the nightmares were worse than the climb.

The moon was more than enough to see by. The cloudy image of Bar-Abba gave way to the focus of the climb. My mind and body were wiped of fear.

Upward progress was slow at first, little strength in my cold body. But the first legs of the climb were easy and, as dawn peaked over the mountains, my purpose and rhythm were roused from deep within me. A simian strength worked into my sinews, and I felt refreshed as my hands found clean, wide holds and my feet danced their way up the face. Cai Lun's training, it seemed, would more than suffice.

I covered the first two hundred pedes of the day in less than an hour. The crack system was expansive on this section. The repeated execution of hand expansions and foot jams was painful but harmonious. The crack ended at a slab of what looked like marble: a perfectly smooth, vertical face. Never a sight a climber wants to see.

I had reached the first crux, blank and featureless, vastly different than the climbing so far. To continue, I had to traverse the marble forty pedes to my right where the crack system continued upward.

The all too familiar beat of my heart rumbled across the valley, and my mind fogged with fear once again. There was nothing beneath my feet but air. The snaking glaciers looked like a strand of hair, thin and distant. I was fifteen hundred pedes high at least. I could see my death three stadium below. If my feet faltered...

Every move across this face had to be perfect.

I jammed my left hand and foot in the crack as far as I could and tightened my pack with one hand. Summing what courage I had, I swung out onto the blank face.

My first handhold was thinner than a coin, offering blinding agony as I put the full weight of my body on it. Only the very tips of my fingers made contact. My right foot found an even smaller chip of rock. I matched hands on the hold and inhaled deeply before pulling my weight sideways and shifting onto my foot. With delicate precision I threw up with my hand over, praying for larger holds, finding more of the same tiny, sharp coins.

The traverse continued with the same handholds and foot placements across the slab, my chest plastered to the wall, steeper and smoother than polished glass. Nothing, I realized, could outwit nature. She did not want me to continue. I did.

It took me half an hour to move thirty pedes, my arms numbed and weakened, fire in my veins. My hands wouldn't close. Every muscle trembled.

Desperation gripped like a vice; my mind darted back to the image of Bar-Abba. He destroyed my family, my lover, and now came for me.

If I did not finish this climb, who would? What man could follow what I'd already climbed? I had no choice but to continue. Failure meant... Suddenly, I heard my voice cry, "I've come too far!"

My answer was silence. My right hand found the final hold, smallest and sharpest yet, and my left hand matched. Five pedes to my right was the end of the traverse, my salvation from this torture of a crack system. But if I pulled down, my fingers were coming off. This was a knife I was gripping. What choice did I have?

With a bitter scream, I pulled onto the razor edge, letting my feet drop, suspended by hands alone. To move on, I had to find foot placements, but there was nothing but slick marble beneath me. With an enormous bellow, I swung my right foot far out to my side, my entire body horizontal. I jammed my foot in the crack and twisted to lock in. My body now splayed sideways—a sacrificial offering to the mountain, my hands gripping the razor-thin hold, my right foot in the crack—I shifted my weight to the right and began fishing my hand toward the crack.

Every muscle begged for relief. They wanted failure, to give in to the mountain. They just wanted to stop. Anything to stop this agony. Even death. The burn spread to my legs. I pulled harder because I had no other option. I pulled because I wanted it.

I could feel my body slowly hinging away from the rock as my right hand blindly searched for a hold. My stomach tightened in anticipation of the fall.

My foot lurched out of the crack, the soles of my boots useless.

I slipped.

My boot peeled away.

With one scream I dropped it all and threw for the crack.

My fingers were in. I was in. I entered the security of the fissure. Instantly, my muscles loosened, my heart slowed, my breathing calmed. I laughed with relief and took a moment to look down again, survey what I had accomplished.

Two thousand pedes below was a sight of infinite humility. Every boulder I staggered over to get here was a tiny imperfection in a plank of wood, the long sheets of glacial ice were the grain; the carpenter was invisible. I understood what Cai Lun was talking about.

From here it looked like I could finish in a few hours, five hundred pedes at most. At the end, a tiny roof capped the finish. From this far away it was hard to measure out just how large the roof was, it could be ten pedes deep or a hundred. I was hoping for ten.

I moved upward again after just a moment's rest with the metered patience and rhythm I had developed over the past two days: hand over hand, foot over foot. Within the next hundred pedes of crack climbing, my arms and legs recovered, but the holds below had cut deeply into my fingers. Blood smeared on the granite as I moved, making the rock slick the moment I touched it.

The crack slowly narrowed, splitting and then running parallel. The system was straight as an arrow, as if a sword had sliced the rock.

The crack grew so narrow only the tips of my fingers could penetrate it, and I had to smear my boots against the face again. I twisted three fingers into the rock and pulled down hard. This move pushed my center of gravity away from the face, putting all the more strain on my torn, bloody fingers.

My focus blurred as agony resurged. My footwork stumbled as if over ice, and desperation returned. Thirty pedes above me, the roof jutted out. A ceiling of stone. I was lucky, it was ten pedes. Ten pedes more between me and the top. But in the wrong direction. On my current path, there was no way around it. I couldn't down climb the way I had come up, and I couldn't traverse left or right without encountering worse problems.

The only route to the summit was through the roof. I had no option but to climb upside down across the ceiling of the roof and pull myself over the lip.

I remembered Mary in the desert, a roof not dissimilar to this one.

She did it…

"And so must you!" I said aloud.

I continued up the crack, moving as quickly as I dared to save strength. My arms numbed, but my will redoubled.

You must finish; retreat is impossible.

Or else what was the point of all this travel, all this searching for… for what?

I reached the lip of the roof where the crack split in two, widening as it moved further out.

I moved my left hand out onto the roof as far as I could and jammed my right foot in behind it, committing to the overhang. As I hung there, upside down, the wind picking up my hair, the sun casting an infinite shadow into the valley below, fear left me. Only the task ahead remained. Five stadium lay between me and the valley. I was exposed; the air that no other man had breathed lay below me, and nothing else. This world was mine.

Climbing upside down was harder than my first day with Cai Lun. One move was the sum total of my remaining will. Sweat pooled in my eye sockets, and dripped down my brow. I imagined it landing a milliarium into the snowfield below, making shattering smack that no living thing would hear.

I screamed with every move. The ten pedes of climbing took only moments, but time slowed. Days had past in this desolate void, hours flying by like the currents in a river. Now, in this peril, a moment was a lifetime. To finish was a move away, and a move was farther than the trek I had yet endured.

I reached the lip of the roof, the end. A rock larger than any I had encountered thus far, large enough to take the entire width of my hand, was there to greet me. I let my body fall out of the crack and hang from the lip. In one swift movement, I threw my left foot as high as my shoulder, found another rock as large as the other. Just as I transitioned my weight, I heard a crack. The sound soared through the air as fast as the pain ripped through my body. My arm wouldn't move. My shoulder had dislocated.

With a flash of strength and a final panicked scream, I managed to get my entire body in line with the torn shoulder, and put all my weight on both feet.

I was now standing on the roof. The summit was a short walk on snow. Without thinking, my body moved forward, wanting nothing more than to be finished. My limp, useless right arm flopped at my side. I walked the last few pedes and slumped my broken body on the summit.

I was done. My body destroyed. My arm lifeless. Only one desire left in my mind: sleep.

But I knew I had to reset my shoulder. I slammed into the ground, jamming the ball joint back into its socket. The pain was beyond anything my mind or body could comprehend. I collapsed in the mushroom cap of snow on the peak of the nameless tower. My task complete, I shut my eyes and slept, the right half of my body buried in snow.

Chapter 10

I awoke beneath a quarter moon. I didn't know how much time had passed, lying there in the snow, broken and useless, but alive.

My entire right side was numb, the cold temporary relieving the pain, granting me the strength to continue. I stood up to marvel at my accomplishment and realized I was far from finished.

The tower knife-edged fifty pedes to my left, quickly dropping into the valley below. From this height, I could see Kechu in all its glory, the peak of the great beyond. Further north was the Han empire. A beautiful sight but no help to my descent.

My journey lay below me, a living map of how far I had come. I stood on an island amidst a sea of endless, unforgiving granite, bathed in moonlight. My heart was calm, my mind quiet. Yet in all of the glory of this peak I saw the new path that lay before me, as treacherous and dangerous as that which I had just finished.

My ascent, my triumph was only the beginning.

Now I had to get down.

Panic, desperation, fear? They are simple enough to handle while climbing. But standing still allows the full weight of those emotions to bare.

I had to descend back along the path I had just destroyed my body to ascend. There was no way, I thought, I could descend the same route I had just climbed. But if I wanted to live, I had to get back to Goktas, to Cai Lun. If I wanted to live, I had to make my way back somehow.

This Cai Lun had failed to train me for.

The southern face, though more featured than my climb, was still vertical, too vertical for any sort of down climb. I was left with two options: to reverse my route, one in which I was barely able to go up, or to skirt north and hope I found a way back to the river and Cai Lun.

The north face was angled, slabby but not too steep. It brought to mind a door stop. This route looked bare and without places to stop, but it looked less dangerous than the way I'd come. If I were to commit to this way down, it would be without break, one continuous down climb from peak to floor.

Do you have it in you? Do you have a choice?

The moon was bright enough to light my path, and I wanted to take full advantage of the numbness the snow gifted my shoulder. I set off down the north face in a rush. My climb up was about careful footwork and precise movement. This climb down would be more reckless. I just wanted to be down, to be done.

I sat on the edge of the cliff, gathered my courage, aimed at the only ledge I could see, and started sliding. My speed careened out of control, sending me down much faster than I'd expected. I slammed my feet down hard trying to slow my slide.

In a few moments I hit the ledge and stopped cold. From here to the valley floor there would be no more ledges to catch me. If I were to come to a patch of ice or slick rock, there would be nothing to stop me from joining the birds, yet no other option remained. My journey was far from over and I was not going to let it end here. I continued my slide down into the valley, down into the dark.

I slid fifty pedes, one hundred, two hundred. After another three hundred pedes, I was a third of the way down, a third of the way done. I could see the chunk of ice that fell my first day, it glowed blue among the granite boulders. The ice was small from here but visible, about the head of a nail.

As I slid, the face grew steeper and slicker, and I picked up speed, my boots doing little to slow my pace. My eyes shot to the ice again; all I could think about was how much larger it was getting. Bigger than a coin now. The size of a hammer. I could make out the huge cracks scarring the ice from the fall. It was getting too big too fast.

At fifteen hundred pedes my boots were smoking but doing nothing. I slapped behind me, searching for a hold to catch myself. The ice was bigger than my head and growing. New fissures in the granite appeared to my right and left, shooting by like arrows as I fell. Now the ice was larger than a house. I forced my hands out to either side, finding whatever purchase I could in the rock scars. I managed, I don't know how, to bridge my body in a chimney and slow my fall. Still about the size of a house, it wasn't growing as fast. Skin sheared from my hands as I slowed. I felt the blood pool on my palms but pushed out harder, screaming as flesh flayed off, like skin from a rabbit

My fall stopped.

I was now hanging; face out, my bloodied hands gripping rock to my sides. The numbness in my shoulder was gone; I could feel every torn muscle throbbing. The ice was still the size of a house, maybe a Roman house, but not getting bigger. I pushed my hands hard to the side, thankful I wasn't moving. I looked up and could barely make out the summit; I must have slid two thousand pedes in less than three minutes.

Outside the chimney was another crack. It looked like it ran the entire height of the face to the valley floor. I slapped for a fist jam inside and pulled out of the chimney. Jamming foot after foot, bloody hand after bloody hand, I descended another five hundred pedes—totally exhausted—down the face. My arms began to burn and weaken again, drawing much-needed strength. My twisted and beaten ankles grew lifeless, my feet dangling from them like fish on a stringer.

My right side was now dead weight, another obstacle in the constant barrage. The peace I'd found on the ascent vanished. I thought about a warm bed, water, food, getting back to Cai Lun. I wanted nothing more than to be done with this place, with this beautiful torture. The crack terminated at a patch of snowpack. There was no other section to climb, only the snow that led to the base. The pain in my hands and shoulder drove me downward. I had to get off this mountain. I leapt onto the snowpack and off the climb.

At last the base of the tower.

Flat, solid earth. Rest. Survival.

It had all come.

I fell to my knees in front of the fallen ice.

The chunk was large, much larger than it looked from above. I had seen drawings of Solomon's Temple when I was a child. This ice was at least as big—a temple in its own might. Behind the ice was the obelisk of the nameless tower.

A full day and night had passed, at least, since I stood on the summit. I saw the shadow of the tower cast into the valley, unmistakable in shape. The mountain had allowed me to live. I could not have been more grateful. If true reverence had not existed for me yet, it was now in abundance.

I washed my hands of blood with snow and walked to the valley floor. The sun was up, filling the valley with a ripe glow and warming my face.

Morning had come, as it always does.

I turned one final time but the nameless tower was hidden behind cliffs. That obelisk slept eternally, obscured from man.

The hike back to Goktas took three days. I made it with ease.

I found Cai Lun sitting, much as I had left him, gnawing on fresh quail. He had prepared a meal for me, not a shred of surprise on his face

86

as I approached, only a smile. He held out a spit of fowl, knowing I would be ready to eat. It had been a week since I left. In that time I had barely eaten, let alone on fire-roasted quail.

"Did you find what you were looking for?" he asked. He spoke as if our conversation had never stopped, as if I'd been with him here the whole time.

I tore into the quail, a ravenous mutt finally fed. Cai Lun graced me a few moments to myself.

"Nothing is as it seems," I responded between gnaws on bone. "The world around us is simply here, not for man alone. The tower will be there forever. I will live but a blink in comparison."

The meat was juicy, and I savored the marrow left in the tiny bones.

"As you said, few venture into those great mountains, yet there they stood. They are simply there," I said.

Cai Lun pulled out his small coin and idly played with it, turning it fast between his fingers as I continued to eat and talk.

How was he able to do that?

"The mountain fights because we fight her." My thoughts coalesced into perfect focus as I spoke. "Fighting against such a force is foolish. I can only turn my face against the injuries and press on."

"Did you find truth in the mountains?"

The coin shot out of sight and reappeared in the other hand.

"No," I said. "I found myself."

The coin disappeared with a spark and reappeared in my own hand, pressing against the quail bone in my palm.

"Judging by the smile on your face and your injuries," he continued, "you did indeed climb something dangerous. This is no small feat."

Cai Lun walked to the cart to retrieve a thick cloth and ointment. He dressed the wounds covering most of my body and delicately wrapped my right arm in a sling.

I pushed the coin hard into my skin as he worked.

"What you have accomplished is tantamount to divine; to overcome such constant suffering is testament to the human condition. It really is short of a miracle you survived, Jiu Zhu."

I stood fast and dropped the coin.

"You sent me there to die?"

He pushed me back down and began to rub salve onto my

shoulder, his strong hands finding and repairing torn sinew.

"No. I sent you there to see."

"I'm proud of what I've done but...what did you find when you did this?"

Cai Lun stopped his massage.

"I never said I climbed the nameless tower. I tried. I found it and I stood in awe at its beauty. But that was it. I spent two weeks at the base. I tried everything I could think of to pluck up the courage to climb."

"But you never climbed it?!" I couldn't believe it. The only thing that kept me going was the knowledge he'd done the same thing before me.

"No," he answered. "I never did. But does it matter?"

I shrugged his hands off my back and turned to glare into his eyes. "Yes! It matters."

Cai Lun put more salve on his hands and turned me back around, forcing the massage to continue.

"The only truth, the only belief that matters, is belief in one's self," he said. "What difference does it make that I didn't have your courage, your resolve?"

Cai Lun's admission was infuriating, but the man's faith in my ability was without end. It dawned on me that he gleaned a greater purpose I did not yet know. Cai Lun was right: belief is what carries you through, faith in yourself and nothing more. What else was there?

"Cai Lun...the world is not what I thought it was," I said.

He pushed down on my shoulder; the pain was intense but healing. I looked down when he stopped rubbing and the coin was back in my hand.

"Neither are you," he said.

Chapter 11

Every moment I spent with Cai Lun I loved. He was my mentor and my teacher, but, more than anything, he was my friend. He never called me anything but Jiu Zhu or little Jew, and took a long time before he told me why.

From Goktas, we reversed along the trade routes, stopping in Kashi where we learned about the new Han empire. Wang Mang had been slowly losing power. Farmers in the south, with weapons from General Liu Xiu, were rebelling against him. They saw the cultivation of a free empire as a threat to their way of life. Ziying was right about Liu Xiu: he was moving in and Cai Lun couldn't have been happier. If Liu Xiu claimed the throne, Cai Lun could be in a better position than when he left; he could take back his old life.

I wanted to think we moved east for a grander purpose, that Cai Lun's passions had been reignited, but it was his pride that drove him east. I still had much to learn, and the thought of Bar-Abba shivered my bones. I wasn't ready to go home, so I followed.

It took another four weeks across open desert to reach Anxi. In the old Han, Anxi was the furthest outpost. Cai Lun figured that if we arrived, his position next to Liu Xiu would be assured. As we moved closer, Cai Lun's mind turned to trickery, and my teachings moved toward the tradecraft by which he earned his place in the Han empire: entertainment and wonder.

I did not begrudge Cai Lun for treating me as an assistant, but the tricks seemed childish compared to his teachings in Goktas. His sorcery was sleight of hand and careful planning, nothing more. The goal of his magic was less to entertain and more to exaggerate truth. His goal was to instill doubt. The coin trick was the first I learned. Though I'm not sharing the secrets, it was painfully obvious when he told me.

I saw his schemes and appreciated them for what they were. I learned much on that road, not all from Cai Lun.

We stopped early that day, typically pushing late into the night. The road was harsh desert between Kashi and Anxi. It'd been two weeks and everyone was tired. Cai Lun had been feverishly working on something in the back cart, leaving me to tend to the horses. Something for Liu Xiu's army. I could hear his clanking bottles and vulgar disappointment even over Aesop whining. The horse had hurt its hind leg and wouldn't stop limping. I pulled over and made camp when I couldn't take Aesop's sad face anymore.

It took Cai Lun another three hours before he joined me; I spent the time consoling poor Aesop.

"Little Jew, look!" Cai Lun said as he approached the camp fire. The moon full but pale, only offering enough light to pick up movement.

Cai Lun dropped a handful of dust into the flames. The fire burst twenty pedes in the air, singeing my beard. I jumped back before the flames took the rest of me.

"What was that?"

Cai Lun could not help his smile.

"I caught your imagination didn't I?"

"And?" I asked.

"It's a particularly effective concoction, primarily of brimstone. Now bear with me, my idea for this concoction is a little ouroboric…" His smile turned sour.

"Cai Lun?"

He stared. A long chain of events passed through his mind. That much was clear.

"…this is not good," he finally said, looking at the powder in his hands.

That was it. No deeper questioning. No philosophical argument on the ramifications of his invention. It was as if, in that moment, he realized what the powder was, or could be, and regretted ever creating it.

But not all his inventions were so dangerous. He taught me a many tricks of healing as well.

After my climb, Cai Lun helped me get through the worst of the recovery. For weeks my injuries from the nameless tower left my hands and shoulder useless. When I couldn't manage, Cai Lun would rub salve into my hands. My shoulder needed something stronger and stranger.

Cai Lun was a teacher of demonstration, not tradition. He wanted me to learn on my own. We were still far from any outpost, two weeks out of Kashi. He had massaged salve on me every night since the climb, but this was the first time he brought out the needles.

"Your shoulder," Cai Lun said as he arranged a jar of needles on a stone, "has been pulled from the joint. You managed to get it back in, but you left a fair amount of internal damage. "

"But I reset my shoulder weeks ago." The needles were as long as daggers. "What are you going to do with those?" I asked, my eyes widening with apprehension.

A smile spread across his face. "Worry not, little Jew. I am going to insert these needles into your skin. This won't cure you, but it will help. You are going to need regular training to really get better."

"Exercise and getting stabbed. That's going to help? I've lost most of the strength in my right arm. I figured it was gone for good."

He gave me a nod, as if to say it would be fine. "Take off your shirt."

It was windy that night, stronger than most desert breezes. He had to keep blowing the sand off the needles before we could start. The anticipation was maddening.

When the wind had calmed enough for Cai Lun to begin, he inserted the tiny needles along my spine, face, shoulder, and legs. The sensation of hundreds of tiny pin pricks was oddly calming once the fear wore off. I laughed at myself: after the nameless tower, I should be fearless.

"I saw your face, little Jew, before I began. You were terrified. You still don't trust me, do you?" His smile grew larger as he worked. "Trust me. In time it will help."

My shoulder did heal. It took the entire trip and countless sessions with the needles, but, eventually, it healed.

We arrived in Anxi after thirty-two days in the desert, and I was glad to be out of the sand. The outpost was small, similar to Merv, but the gates entering were solid Jade and made no noise as they swung open before us. This area of the world had seen far fewer conquerors than the west. The Han emperors had been here for a long time, and few had dared challenge them.

Anxi was a crossroads and a garrison along the massive wall built by the old Han emperors. This wall protected citizens from nomadic tribes to the south and west. From the Jade gate of Anxi, the wall stretched unbroken, all the way to the Han capital of Chang'an, five hundred milliaria away. Standing thirty pedes high, and ten pedes deep, it was a testament to the power of the Dynasty.

Entrance into the town was blocked by guards, but Cai Lun greeted them like friends. The men were skeptical at first, impressed by westerners with a mastery of the language but doubtful of our alleged connection to the emperor. We spent the night outside the gates, allowing the men time to consider. At dawn they let us through.

Cai Lun was anxious to return to Chang'an, the Han capital, so we resumed our journey as soon as the guards finished checking us out.

They explained that Liu Xiu had removed Wang Mang from the throne and had immediately instructed the occupation of all military outposts, a fact the soldiers of Anxi seemed none too pleased with. The news drove Cai Lun onward, setting the horses at a full gallop before the soldiers could tell us the whole story.

The road from Anxi to Chang'an was well paved. What would have taken another month on open terrain took a few days. Aesop and Agape moved toward the capital with as much enthusiasm as Cai Lun. They were happy to finally be on pavement again.

Chang'an was a miraculous capital, purposely designed and elegantly executed. But the majesty of the city was only matched by its current desolation. Chang'an was abandoned, in what looked like a hurry. Liu Xiu had relocated the capital to Luoyang, the alleged center of the world, leaving Wang Mang's old capital in disarray. Chang'an had once stood as the center of the Han and the terminus to the trade roads for many hundreds of years. From the exterior, the city looked intact, but as we approached it was obvious it had fallen, as had Cai Lun's spirits.

We entered through the eastern gates, no guards or pomp greeting us. The city was encased in smooth, grey brick, standing thirty pedes at all points and twenty pedes deep. Taller than any tree I had ever seen and four times as thick. Twice the walls of Jerusalem.

The gate fed into the main artery of the city, a causeway a stadium in width that subdivided the city. Smaller, residential roads branched out from this main hub.

Like the spokes on a wagon wheel, this road had eleven just like it, each leading into the palace from one of the primary gates. The avenues were lined with matching fig trees, once pruned to perfection and identical in size, clearly left to their own devices during the city's decline. The groomed nature of Chang'an once made it appear drawn more than built. Chang'an was pulled from the imagination of countless emperors. Now it was desolate, empty, and alone.

We drew closer to the palace, a slow funeral march along deceased corridors.

Left-over families scurried back into their homes, like rats who

92

had not yet deserted the ship. The people were all un-bathed, emaciated, and terrified. We ran into a small girl clutching a porcelain doll. The girl was filthy but the doll was immaculate. It must have cost a fortune. The moment she saw Cai Lun on top of Aesop, she burst into shrill tears and dropped the porcelain figure, shattering it on the pavement. A filthy old man sprinted from a nearby house like a cockroach and pulled the girl back inside. I picked up the remains of the doll and tried to return it, thinking of the babe the Romans left in the streets of my home.

"Jiu Zhu!" Cai Lun barked. "Forget them. We have business here."

He never yells, unless we are training. What's wrong?

The palace sat above the rest of the city, obscured from sight, a broken mast peaking above a sunken ship. We could see it from the east gates and knew where to go. The main artery of Chang'an terminated in a waterfall of stairs that stretched upward, out of sight. The palace was above.

"How many steps are there?" I asked, slack-jawed.

Cai Lun motioned for us to continue, silent.

Hewn from flawless marble, the steps protected the emperor from anyone less than motivated.

We tied the cart and horses to a large scholar tree and ran up the stairs. Cai Lun was silent, breathless. Since he had heard news of Liu Xiu's return, he had driven toward this palace with the fervor of a man obsessed. Reaching his destination to see it destroyed gripped him like a sickness.

We reached the top of the steps after several minutes. The outer walls of the palace rose into view as if from the stairs themselves: higher than the city walls yet more delicate, more decorated. The walls were lined with jade dragon figures and painted with a dark lacquer. The only flaw was the main gate composed of the same white marble as the steps. In front sat a single guard, hooded and cloaked.

Cai Lun approached the vagabond and kowtowed. "We seek entrance into this kingdom, and ask your permission to continue."

I had never heard him speak with such respect, particularly to a squatter.

The vagabond lowered his head, further obscuring his face, and spoke in a practiced, yet broken tongue.

"Permission has fled from this city, as have all masters. This wasteland is all that remains. Who are you?"

The tone of the squatter forced Cai Lun back into a speechless stupor. I stood there, quietly observing the two, sensing I had missed an important social cue. Cai Lun swayed back and forth as though drunk. I took over, bowing to the man but not as deeply.

"We seek audience with the grand emperor of the new Han kingdom. We are friend to the court."

The squatter stood, threw his hood, and thrust a sword to my throat in one swift movement. His hands were trembling.

"The Han kingdom has fallen! This is all that is left!"

I raised my hands in surrender. "I mean you no harm my friend and I didn't mean to offend. We will leave. It was our mistake coming."

In a flash, Cai Lun grabbed the man, disarmed and pinned him to the ground. His knee was pressed against the squatter's throat, pressing so hard he turned red.

"Who are you to threaten my journey, to raise a sword against us? What gives you the right?"

The man broke into maniacal laughter, through choked breaths. "What gives me the right?" He cackled deeper. "I am the king!"

Cai Lun's eyes widened, but he did not remove his knee. "Liu Xiu's men killed Wang Mang. Who are you?"

"I am the emperor and Liu Xiu did nothing," the beggar responded.

Cai Lun stood, threw the sword down the steps, and helped the man to his feet.

"How did you escape the destruction of the city?"

The emperor put his hood back on and opened the massive gates without an answer.

Cai Lun turned to me. "I am not sure this man is who he claims to be. Keep an eye on him; he may have other weapons hidden."

I nodded as we walked through.

The interior courtyard of the palace was as deserted as the rest of the city, if not untouched. Two chestnut trees stood at the center, bark twisted wildly, surrounded on all sides by smooth marble. The interior walls were as lacquered as the exterior, cast in shadow by the overhangs protecting them. Behind the chestnuts stood the imperial residence. It was raised on a second wave of marble steps. A throne of jade sat outside the entrance. The jade had been scratched and broken in multiple places, a slab from the top sat strewn to the side.

Our escort climbed the steps, shuffled inside, and disappeared. After a few minutes, the man called for us to enter, irritated we weren't already there.

The house was the epicenter of Chang'an's destruction. It was as if the men who had ransacked the city focused all their energy on this one building. A flurry of action had thrown lacquered wood in piles throughout the house. Discarded arrowheads, swords, and broken daggers littered the back wall. Pools of rancid blood still soaked the floor. Graffiti had been hewn into the wood walls. A practiced hand had drawn the characters, one adept at blade work and lettering. It read: *The House of Jujun*. Beneath the inscription was the old king's chamber pot, un-emptied, defecation piling up. The beggar had constructed a makeshift throne out of broken tables, but this man was no carpenter. The heap of wood seemed held together by little more than its own weight. On the edge of the throne, the vagabond hung a cloth crown, tied together from torn gowns and simple knots. It looked like something a child would make when dressing up as Caesar. A madman would not take the time to move up here to the palace; it was in worse shape than the city below. Only someone with a connection to this house would stay…that or a self-deprecating recreant. It seemed the man before us was both. It had to be Wang Mang. I looked to Cai Lun. I could see he had just come to the same realization. He wasn't angry for the previous attack anymore, only sympathetic.

Next to the woodpile was a small fire, circled by broken marble chips. The squalor in which this man lived provided great contrast to the former glory of this house. It was a pathetic sight to see Wang Mang in this pigsty of a home. This beggar really was the old king.

I couldn't help but feel pity as well. At times it seemed the beggar had accepted the fall of his dynasty; moments later, anger would shoot back into his brow. He was torn, struggling with a demon deep inside. Wang Mang sat at a crossroads between broken dreams and the inability to let them go. His house reeked of regret.

"Welcome to the House of Jujun," Wang Mang said with a listless bow.

He grabbed the silk crown and jammed it over his hood.

I looked to Cai Lun, worried. He was more than sympathetic. His face was red from holding back the shared pain.

Before breaking into tears, Wang Mang ripped off the crown and tossed it into the flames. The silk started to smoke and wilt. The final straw had broken.

"Wang Mang, what happened here?" Cai Lun asked.

He took time to gather the fractures of his mind.

"I just wanted to be happy, my people to be happy. The child emperor wanted fun...war."

He blew his nose into the soiled rags of his coat.

"Would you give a sword to a child?"

He looked at us wide eyed. Did he want an answer?

Cai Lun moved in closer. He stoked the fire and began rubbing the shoulders of the king.

"Who would give an empire to a child?" Wang Mang asked. "When the Kushans started to attack in full, what was I supposed to do? Did the empire want a ten year old to fend off a savage horde? When Kujula Kassa took over the army, it got worse. The Kushans threatened everything. I had to act."

The confession poured out, blood from an open wound, as Cai Lun rubbed away the old king's woes.

How can he stand to be in here with this smell?

I wanted to leave. The smell grew stronger as I stood in it. It was difficult to breathe. The pools of blood were the worst offenders, like a butcher shop that had been abandoned. I felt like I was going to get a disease just being in there.

Wang Mang's affect softened as Cai Lun massaged and I grew sicker. "The land is saturated, it can hold no more. No more blood," he sighed sadly.

Cai Lun moved to Wang Mang's side and stared. He wanted to share what he could of the emotional load. Wang Mang could not bear it alone. He cried with the king.

"I was friends with Liu Xiu. Now this," Wang Mang said. His voice was hard to hear and understand, a whimpering child unable to speak.

Cai Lun pulled the beggar into a hug.

Wang Mang recoiled when he was touched. He turned and shot Cai Lun a piercing look, the first eye contact he made with us. He looked like a dog beaten one too many times.

I jumped back to the entrance; I did not want this mad mongrel to attack again. Cai Lun stayed where he was. He forced his arms around Wang Mang and hugged harder.

His face did not soften; it was blood red and frothing. Cai Lun looked like he was trying to hold a furious hyena in place. I moved closer to the door.

Wang Mang pushed him off, his face blank now. The anger had disappeared like Cai Lun's magic coin. He reached into the flames and unflinchingly pulled out the molten crown. He put it on his head and sauntered to the corner.

"Cai Lun, he's mad. Let's go," I said.

I could smell the heat of the fabric burning his flesh and scorching hair. The beggar just stood there, facing the corner, silent.

Cai Lun glanced at me in defeat. "You are right. We should go. There is nothing for us now."

Wang Mang began muttering to himself. "House of Jujun... House of jujun...House of jujun. House of jujun house of jujun house of jujun house of jujun," his voice rising hysterically as he screamed into the corner.

"House of jujun house of jujun house of jujun house of jujun house of jujun house of...."

"Jiu Zhu, we need to leave!" Cai Lun had to yell over his screaming.

Wang Mang started banging his head against the wall. Hard. Fast. The muttering climaxed as blood started spraying over the back of his head.

We sprinted out the gate and through the pristine courtyard, down the endless steps, back to Aesop and Agape.

Chapter 12

We left Chang'an in a hurry. Based on what we gleaned on the road, Luoyang was only three days away. If Cai Lun wanted to be back in the glory of the Han we would have to go there. A piece of Cai Lun was left with Wang Mang; much of his egotism had vanished. We rode for Luoyang not because Cai Lun wanted to be respected but because we set out to do so. Now it was about finishing what we started.

We reached Luoyang quickly. It was less impressive than Chang'an but newer. It looked more like a bloated garrison, brimming with soldiers and machines of war. It was a city built for war and the new capital of the Han.

Liu Xiu, the new king, was concerned with regaining control of the empire. Military presence increased the closer we drew to the city center. Our small cart had to pass through thirty checkpoints before reaching the outer walls and another dozen to enter the inner city. Cai Lun's military identification was still valid in this new empire, smoothing our entry, but the new king was cautious.

Louyang's palace was a shadow of that in Chang'an with a thatched roof, bamboo supports, and linen walls. Liu Xiu was not concerned with accommodations. His task was to bring unification back to the Han.

The head royal guard was an old comrade of Cai Lun's. He recognized our horses as we rode closer to the palace gates and sent a party to escort us. Cai Lun may have been a court wizard by trade, but his connection to the inner circle made us well received. We were taken to the imperial chambers as soon as we passed the final checkpoint.

When we arrived at the royal chambers, Cai Lun's friend stopped us. "I know you two were friends before the rise of the new Han," he said. "The emperor is a busy man though. Please be patient and try not to make much noise."

At that he notified the court steward and left.

Despite their old ties, even Cai Lun had to stand in line to see the king.

"Jiu Zhu," he said after the steward left, "Liu Xiu is a patient man, patient and proud. You are an outsider. Men from the west rarely come here, making you a bit of an attraction. I am hoping you can become friends with the emperor. Try to use his delight at your presence to your advantage. Impress Liu Xiu. Press your luck with his willingness to entertain a novelty such as yourself."

I gave Cai Lun a quizzical look. "You think...you think I can be friends with the Han despot?"

He turned toward me, panicked. "Do *not* use that word. He may have deposed Wang Mang, but Wang Mang had no authority to rule." He paused. "And, yes, I think you can be friends."

A group of guards streamed past, throwing open the small tarp that protected the emperor's chamber. Something urgent was happening, but I soon learned this was always the case in such an embattled kingdom.

"Cai Lun?" I asked cautiously. "I have never spoken to a king before. I am not sure how to act."

He shot me a surprised look. "You had never climbed a mountain either. Look how well that turned out." Then he paid me a kind smile. "And Kujula is a king, of sorts. I am sure you will do fine."

A short man threw open the linen tarp, a worried expression as he spoke to a group of guards. The look faded when he noticed Cai Lun.

"Cai Lun!" he said. "Is that you?"

Cai Lun gave the man a hug, saying, "I'm back!" as he slapped him on the shoulder.

"Where have you been?" the short man asked.

Cai Lun shrugged. "This is my new apprentice."

He motioned for me to join them. I bowed. The small man was surprised to see me as well.

"Jiu Zhu," Cai Lun said, "this is emperor Liu Xiu."

"Jiu Zhu!" the emperor laughed. "Making up more fantastical names for our western guests. I suppose it's better than Cai Lun."

Liu Xiu was a practical man; he dressed in imperial garb only for ceremony, preferring a simple, button down robe at all other times. He was young and un-weathered by his duties. I noted how calm and patient his speech was the moment he opened his mouth.

"Who is he, Cai Lun? A man of the west? From the looks of his hair, Rome or somewhere near?" Liu Xiu asked, assuming I did not speak the language.

"As he said, I am Cai Lun's assistant," I answered out of turn.

Both men stopped in their tracks.

"You speak our language perfectly," Liu Xiu responded. "I can see Cai Lun has taken a clever man as his assistant."

Cai Lun looked worried. He hadn't realized what initiative I would take.

"Yes, he is indeed," Cai Lun said, grabbing my hand tight, trying to reclaim control of the conversation. "But, Liu Xiu, how is the empire?"

The emperor became irritated. "You are not an advisor yet, my friend, and I am done with work today. Please, Jiu Zhu," he chuckled again. "Tell me about yourself."

I pressed hard into Cai Lun's grip. Cai Lun had asked me to make friends, and I was planning to do just that.

"Have you ever played lantrunculi emperor?" I asked.

Liu Xiu's eyes opened wide. He shuffled to a small drawer next to his bedside, and took out a playing board and pieces. In the center of the room was a table cluttered with maps and tea cups. With one sweep, Liu Xiu cleared the table, sending the debris to the floor, and began setting his side of the board.

I looked to Cai Lun. I knew I did not need his permission but wanted to regain whatever face I lost. He was not pleased but nodded gently.

"I can see you two will be busy; Jiu Zhu is quite a player," he said. "Liu Xiu, is Fubo still your number one?"

"General Fubo now, and yes. Though you are not likely to find him anywhere but on the battlefield."

"I will leave you two to it then." At that, Cai Lun rushed out and Liu Xiu invited me to play.

"Jiu Zhu, have you served in your king's army?" he asked with a smile as I sat and arranged my pieces.

Cai Lun had recarved the pieces I lost in Seleucia, taking care to replicate them exactly. He gave them to me soon after I finished the nameless tower. It was a graduation present of sorts. With my new pieces and my old dux, I felt back on my game. I took a moment and closed my eyes, recalling every possible move I could think of and Liu Xiu's responses.

"My king?" I paused, realizing my rudeness in answering so slowly. "My king is a puppet of Rome, and the soldiers of Rome serve only themselves."

"Truly? That is very different than the people of the Han." He placed his dux and nodded for me to make the first move.

"That is an interesting piece, Emperor, what is it?" I asked.

Liu Xiu retrieved his dux, and held it up to the dim firelight. "My king. We call them kings in Han Chinese not the Latin dux." He stumbled over the western pronunciation. "It's made from the finger bone of Emperor Gaozu, our first emperor. Over two hundred years ago."

His other pieces were carved to exacting precision. The pawns were pewter and the others brass. The level of detail in each piece was astounding; I could easily pick out the beard hairs on his priests. The dux was comparatively dull. It was little more than a sphere of porcelain-colored bone.

I moved my first pawn out, d4, and nodded to Liu Xiu.

Liu Xiu mirrored the move, sending his pawn to d5.

"As I was saying," he continued. "Soldiers here serve a greater good, and I serve those who serve. Though I am the commander-in-chief, I see myself as a servant."

My second pawn to c4. His to c6 without a blink.

"A servant?" I asked. Third pawn to e3.

"Yes," he answered. His solider danced onto the board at f6.

My solider to c3.

It was clear we were evenly matched.

"My vision has always been to bring a land free of foreign invaders," he said. His dux's pawn moved to e6. "My people do not need a ruler; they need a king. A king who will serve them so that they can rule themselves."

My second soldier to f3.

"But it is you who has gone to war, not your people," I said.

He marshaled a defense with a second solider at d7, his dux now completely impenetrable.

Clever and quick! He knows how to protect what matters.

"You think you can create an empire through blood? Wang Mang gave up his war against the Kushan; you escalated it tenfold."

His face scowled, but he did not look up.

My priest to d2.

He breathed slowly, metering his response.

"The men of my army will die for this cause, die without glory, die without honor but for the Han. I count myself fortunate to be among them." His priest to e7.

Liu Xiu manipulated his pieces like a master puppeteer. His skill in deploying the players on the board was only matched by his cavalier and improvisational style of play.

I cannot predict his moves at all...

"You are very good Liu Xiu," I said, trying to play to his vanity and distract him.

"Nonsense. You are a tactical genius. And no bootlicking, please." He waved the thought aside like an insult. "Perhaps you could better serve the empire as my strategist than as Cai Lun's assistant."

Was it really this easy to join this king's court?

My priest to e2.

"Perhaps," I answered. "But I like to think my plans are far from this place."

He looked surprised, but his focus on the game intensified. Pawn takes c4. "What *is* your plan? Do you want to go home? Go back to a Roman fiefdom?"

"Someday," I said. My priest took his pawn, exc4.

What was that? Why did he let me take the piece? A strange sacrifice so early given his skill.

His face cringed when I set the pewter pawn on my side of the board, as if he had lost a real foot soldier in his army.

"Well," pawn to b5, "I imagine the Han and Rome will someday meet. For better or for worse. I hope the soldiers of Rome can serve their empire as we do," he said.

"Probably not," I answered, rescinding my priest to d3. "But that is not my problem. I want to serve the people, the subjects of Rome—not Rome herself."

"You would fit in here, Jiu Zhu. I put the well being of my soldiers above all else. My end goal is to serve the subjects of Han."

His priest to b7.

"If that's true, why have you improved the living conditions of the army and not the farmers?"

My soldier to e4.

He is sure to strike with that bait; no one can resist taking a solider this early.

He looked up from the board for the first time. "You are lucky Cai Lun is your friend. Other rulers might consider your question treason."

He moved a low pawn to a6, refusing the bait.

"I apologize grand emperor," I said, worried I might have ruined my welcome. I responded with a weak move: pawn to a3.

"No need! No need. We are equals here..."

Black soldier takes mine, fxe4.

The game went on for hours, another hundred moves. I would take a piece, and Liu Xiu would respond by devastating my strategy. Even at the end, I could never discern what he would do next. Despite his unscripted yet successful style of play, he wore the game on his sleeve. His face fell every time I took a piece. It was as if he had a well of emotion to belie his measured willingness to sacrifice the small trinkets of the game.

In the end, all that was left was my dux, one of his pawns and his "king." We called it a draw after one hundred and fourteen moves. He bowed to me, and said goodnight, leaving the pieces on the board.

Liu Xiu's ideals of service through sacrifice struck a chord. The soldiers of Rome served to earn a living…or because they had been sold as slaves. Kujula Kassa, the leader Liu Xiu feared most, had spoken of his soldiers in much the same way—as servants to a cause. In contrast to the ideals of Liu Xiu, the Kushan warriors seemed to serve the cause of bloodlust despite the vision Kujula had shared with me in Goktas. If Liu Xiu's sentiment carried through to his men, the army called to the brotherhood of service, something altogether different than Rome or the Kushan.

Time passed slowly in Luoyang. Cai Lun and I lived a royal life. I became friends with Liu Xiu and his advisors, just as Cai Lun had hoped.

My counsel with the inner court also drew me close to the Chief General of the Han, General Fubo. He was a man of immense dedication. If Liu Xiu was the thought behind the empire, General Fubo was the hand that carried it out.

Fubo didn't play games and only talked about war. He drank strong liquor and never removed his uniform. He was tall for a man of the Han, standing my height but much broader in the shoulders. He was clean-shaven and wore his thick, raven hair in a knot on top of his head.

Our first meeting was outside the quarters of Liu Xiu. I had been summoned while Liu Xiu and Cai Lun were in counsel. A push into the western reaches of the Han had caused new confrontation with the Kushan. Cai Lun informed the emperor I had met with Kujula in Goktas, and knew his mind. The situation made me uneasy; I had known Kujula as a friend, not as a general.

Before entering the emperor's war chamber, Fubo stopped me. I had been there for months and was not used to being questioned by anyone.

"You have been called to advise military action against an enemy of the state. What information do you have regarding the General of the Kushan, emperor Kujula Kassa? Speak quickly!" Fubo barked.

Kujula!? That unassuming man I met in that moonlit temple in Goktas. What was he to the great Han?

"General Fubo," I started, "I met Kujula in a temple. We talked about religion, not war." I had been Liu Xiu's friend for months after that first night. It was uncommon for anyone in the empire to talk to me with such gruffness.

"The advisor Cai Lun informs this counsel that you have detailed information regarding his military plans. Is this true?"

His temper faded when he realized I would not stand for being in an inquisition. But Fubo acted like my knowledge of a man's ideals could somehow lead to his defeat. To him, any insight was a weakness to be exploited.

"Fubo," I said. He shot me an impertinent look. "Sorry. *General* Fubo, this was nearly a year ago. Kujula shared a vision for the Kushan, and how he dreamt of achieving it. That was it."

"Explain!" Fubo barked.

I wasn't sure what there was to explain. "Well…Kujula's ideals are close to Liu Xiu's. He wants to unite a kingdom, to rid the Kushan of any threats so that his people might simply live. His purpose is not to expand, but to secure his borders."

Fubo seemed pleased.

"Please enter and inform Grand Emperor Guangwu of what you have told me." He opened the inner chamber door.

I looked at Fubo with disbelief. I had provided no information of value, yet I had earned this man's respect and permission to counsel his king. Fubo's measure of a man's worth was how much he had to give to the army. Apparently, I had gifted his army a priceless secret.

Cai Lun and Liu Xiu were huddled over a map at the same table on which we had played lantrunculi. The fire in the corner filled the room with a thick perfume. Cai Lun's face was worried, not from his discussion with the king, but because I was walking into the middle of it. He looked like my father when I worked the lathe.

Liu Xiu was as tired as I had even seen him. "Jiu Zhu! Thanks for coming."

I saw Cai Lun's jaw clench.

Liu Xiu rubbed his eyes and poured a cup of tea. "If you wouldn't mind answering a few questions," he said.

"Of course not," I replied.

Cai Lun pulled out a chair for me and widened his eyes. I knew what those eyes meant; he wanted me to be careful.

"Cai Lun told me you know the leader of the Kushan horde," Liu Xiu said. "He thinks—"

Cai Lun turned to the Emperor, staring blankly.

"Sorry. *I* think," Liu Xiu continued, "you can be of some service in a small problem."

I pulled the map over and poured myself a cup of tea. Han tea was bitter; I always had trouble stomaching the brew. This was a map of Cai Lun's creation; the careful notation of landmarks and the roads west were as obvious as my map of the nameless tower.

"I told Fubo everything I know," I said.

Cai Lun put his palms to his face, his veins expanded from the pressure. It took him a few moments before he said anything else.

"What do you think Kujula wants?" Cai Lun asked.

Liu Xiu smiled, eager to get what he needed.

"Land," I answered.

Cai Lun threw off his hands; his face was visibly red.

I could feel the tension in the room but did not glean exactly what I was now part of.

Liu Xiu pulled the map from me and circled the hot zones where his soldiers and the Kushan were fighting. It was in Han territory, south of Kashi. I knew what the point of this campaign was even before asking. If either empire held that land alone, Parthia would move in and attack.

Cai Lun knew I understood. They were asking me to make the choice.

But why me? I know as much about war as a child.

"We need you because you see things others do not," Liu Xiu said, as if reading my thoughts. "Help us decide where to go with this."

Cai Lun's breathing grew heavy and slow, as if to say: choose wisely.

"We do not need this land," Liu Xiu explained. "In fact, I do not

105

want it. It is all sand and mountains out there. Kashi is far enough north not to be threatened if we retreat."

I looked to Cai Lun for help. He turned away.

I was on my own, just like the tower.

Liu Xiu stared at the map, hoping either it or myself would alleviate his conundrum.

"Kujula wants land," I said. "Give it to him. Take your troops out, send them home. The Kushan forces will not follow."

Liu Xiu looked up from the map. His worry had vanished.

"As you said, you don't want that land anyway," I continued.

I heard Cai Lun's teeth grate but did not break eye contact with the Emperor.

Liu Xiu nodded his head and folded up the map. "Good call, Jiu Zhu. Can I get you something stronger than tea?"

Cai Lun pushed over his chair and walked out without a word.

It took a year before the Han forces were able to secure a retreat. I was right; the Kushan army did not follow. It turned out I was almost always right. Over that year, Liu Xiu called me in to advise dozens of times, but never again with Cai Lun in the room. In the end, the Han lost about a hundred square milliaria of land, and five thousand troops. Fubo estimated the Kushan forces lost triple that, all to make themselves a pretty target for Parthia.

Cai Lun and I were not asked to entertain after that first year; his magic tricks did not seem to captivate Liu Xiu or his court. That meant we spent much of our time idle, only called to work alongside Liu Xiu or Fubo once or twice a month. We never talked about why we advised the king separately or what we said to him. It was a sore point in our friendship.

After that first year, when the two of us did little else but fish and read, we became mutually bored. Cai Lun wanted to train again, like we did in Kashi and Goktas. Liu Xiu and Fubo left us alone. The war with the Kushan had ended and the only threat to the Han was the scattered nomads. The great wall took care of them for the most part. When there was confrontation, Fubo was able to end it quickly. That left peace, idle peace. So we trained.

I loved being back in the simplicity of Cai Lun's tutelage. At first we ran, just as we did in Kashi. It had been a while since either of us had exercised, so it was slow at first.

We took a trip south, into the Gan river basin. This was a sparsely populated area, mostly rice farmers. It was beautiful though: sandstone cliffs thousands of pedes high, deep jungles, and prismatic dunes that looked painted by some invisible hand.

Cai Lun began teaching me how to fight. I knew he had some training in self defense. When he disarmed Wang Mang it was obvious the skill had been honed, but I had no idea just how talented my friend was.

We lived in the Gan river basin for six months, in a small hut on a rice paddy. The farmer knew Cai Lun, or at least heard his name, and was pleased to have us. We spent the days sparring in the mud that filled the fields. At night we helped the farmer make dinner.

The meals were simple. Rice and meat. But Cai Lun was able to make a feast of the most meager ingredients. The farmer's house reminded me of home, and I longed to return for the first time.

"What are we doing here, Cai Lun?" I asked. It was late after a hard day of training, and all three of us were drunk.

Even when he wasn't sober, Cai Lun maintained his enigmatic persona. "Stepping into the unknown," he said.

I laughed and choked down more rice wine. "I feel like we are beyond that now, you and I."

"Do you?" Cai Lun asked. "Because I feel like we have spent nearly two years doing next to nothing. Do you know what you cost Kujula?"

This conversation was a long time coming, and I was not about to have it sober. I poured more rice wine for us both. Cai Lun did not drink.

"Why don't you tell me," I said.

Cai Lun sobered entirely. "You knew exactly what was at stake. When the Han left, Parthia moved in. They captured half the Kushan forces, a quarter more were killed. He was your friend, Jew!"

"He was an enemy of the Han!"

I looked up; his eyes were disappointed.

"Tomorrow we are heading south. There are cliffs in the jungle I would like us both to see."

"Cai Lun, I'm sorry. I didn't mean to yell. I'm drunk."

He walked out without a word.

The morning came with a blinding hangover. I walked out of the

107

farmer's hut to an impatient Cai Lun atop Aesop. He set off at full gallop, leaving me alone with Agape.

"Come on buddy," I said to the horse as we started to follow.

He whinnied disapprovingly.

From the Gan river the jungle grew dense and hot. We took our horses as far as the terrain would allow and then walked the rest. It was another day until Cai Lun stopped or even talked to me.

We had come to a sandstone cliff. The tallest I had seen yet. Fifteen hundred pedes at least. The top half of the cliff bulged out like a fat man's gut.

"This is new to us both," Cai Lun said. "Do you want to go first or second?" He handed me a rope.

"First or second for what?" I asked.

He pulled two pairs of boots out of his pack and handed one to me. They were the same boots I used on the nameless tower.

"To climb?" I asked surprised. "I thought you said you—"

"—that I never have?" he interrupted. "That's right, and you have. That is why we have a rope. Let's go."

He took off toward the base of the cliff like a startled deer. When I caught up he was already climbing.

"Cai Lun wait!" I called up. "Let me go ahead of you."

He climbed fast, reaching the bulge before I could even put my boots on. It reminded me of Mary in the desert, fearless and alone.

I tied the rope to my back and followed.

The climb was hard, but not nearly as difficult as the polished granite I was used to. I climbed as fast as I could to make sure Cai Lun was safe. Every time I got close, he took off and cleared another thirty pedes in moments.

When I reached the top and pulled over, he was there waiting for me. The moment I stood up, he kicked me hard in the chest. I nearly fell back down the cliff.

"What the fuck, Cai Lun!"

"Your whore mother must have been proud to birth such an abomination. I'm sure her nasty little rape was a planned event?" His voice was cold, distant. I'd never heard hate like this before. Not from my friend.

"Cai Lun?"

He backed up and got into position, ready to spar. The top of the cliff was narrow, twenty pedes in every direction. There were puddles of rainwater that made the sandstone slick.

Without even bowing, he came at me again. A wild sweep to my legs sent me to my knees. Cai Lun was fierce, not holding back.

I stood back up, and we fought. The wet sandstone made it hard not to spin after every kick. I was more concerned with falling off than fighting, but Cai Lun was focused, enraged. He attacked, blind to everything around him.

A high knee to my face made me black out for a moment. He closed the gap between us after landing and slammed my head against the wet stone like a ravenous monkey cracking a coconut.

I threw him off and backed way up. *What was his problem?* I did not want to hurt my friend, but he had come unhinged. I had to fight just as hard to keep him from killing me.

It was an hour before we stopped. Cai Lun collapsed, near the back edge. His brow was soaked with sweat. I had drawn blood at his lip and eye. I could feel a pool of the same at the back of my head where he had slammed me on the stone.

"Why are we here, Cai Lun?" I yelled.

"Because we were friends!" he looked up and yelled back.

He pulled his knife and threw it like a dart to my face, missing me by a hair's breadth.

"Cai Lun, stop!"

He came at me with a volley of blows, all of which I was able to block. We were beyond tired. His technique was sloppy, and I was confused. Blood and sweat splashed into my face as he continued to punch.

I grabbed his hands, grappled him to the ground, and pressed my knee into his throat.

"Stop this!" I said.

He threw me off and stood up.

We stared each other down, catching our breath.

"Do you know what Jiu Zhu means?" he asked, menace in his eyes.

"No!"

"Savior…" he said. "No one ever uses the word because there isn't a Han who cares about anything but themselves. What you told Liu Xiu that night was wrong; you led thousands of men to their deaths."

What? I had no idea.

"You told me the first night we got to Luoyang to make friends," I said, ashamed of what Cai Lun revealed.

"You are smarter than that," he bellowed back. "You think you can trust every friend you meet?"

I looked at him, confused and sad that I had disappointed him.

He picked up on it and softened slightly. "Ziying. Remember her? She runs a slave whore house out of that inn. I've been friends with that ugly bitch for years. I wouldn't trust her any farther than I can throw her."

He walked over and picked his knife back up. "And Mithra, your little thief comrade who sold you out to Kurush, that sodomite fuck. I've known those two for almost a decade. How do you think I found you rotting in that prison so fast?"

He had nicked the edge of his knife and grunted with frustration. "There are enemies all around you, all of which you need to keep as close as friends. If you want to save anything, you are going to have to figure out which ones you can trust and which ones will kill the thousands that get in their way."

His faced relaxed after a moment of calm breathing. He sighed deeply and bowed. "You said you wanted to figure out how to make peace, not war. You messed up this year, Jiu Zhu." He closed his eyes, sheathed his knife, and came over to hug me. "Come on. Let's go."

Finally.

"Were we training or just letting off steam?" I asked jokingly.

"Little bit of both. You really pissed me off, little Jew." He threw a sweaty arm around my shoulder and walked with me to the edge. "Time to go down."

"And how are we going to do that?" I asked.

"With the rope."

He pulled it off my back and tied it around a rock close to the edge.

As abruptly as the fight started, it ended. Cai Lun did what he needed to do. He threw the rope over the edge and jumped down after it.

Chapter 13

We spent another year and a half traveling between Luoyang and the Gan river valley. The farmer, Houng, was always delighted when we showed up. He had built a modest addition to his hut just for Cai Lun and me. Houng bought a dog to keep us company while he worked the fields. I suspected he needed the company as well. It was a wrinkly Shar Pei puppy named Gofu. We found Houng dead the third summer we made the journey. He was ninety, and must have died in his sleep. Gofu was next to his bed, affectionately licking his swollen hand. We never made it back to the Gan valley after that, but Cai Lun brought Gofu back to our house in Louyang.

After that day in the mountains, Cai Lun and I never fought again. He taught me how, I bested him, and that was enough. We didn't argue, we didn't quarrel. We trained, drank, talked, and wrestled with Gofu. I played lantrunculi with Liu Xiu when we were home and enjoyed my friend when we were away. Since I arrived, Luoyang shed its Spartan style and blossomed into a city as beautiful as Chang'an.

My friendship with Cai Lun grew most of all. We were like brothers: rarely apart and always on each other's minds. I never stopped looking at this man as a teacher. He told me secrets, darker than most can share. I loved Cai Lun even more for his confessions. To admire a man for his strengths is common; to love a man for his weakness is an attribute we could all do better to hone.

As quickly as my relationship with Cai Lun began, one day, it ended.

In an autumn like the first I spent in Luoyang, Cai Lun told me a secret he had long kept.

We were up on the parapets of Liu Xiu's palace. It was a far seeing place we both loved. Our secret meeting spot and no larger than the top of that sandstone cliff we fought on years ago.

Cai Lun was looking over the edge of the tower. He started talking the moment I walked out onto the deck. Gofu ran up and licked my paw when he noticed I had arrived.

"Jiu Zhu, you paid your debt to me a long time ago. I kept you here," he continued, "because it has been years since I have had a friend."

"Cai Lun..." I walked next to him and looked down on the city.

The towers were higher than they used to be, fifty pedes now. A man would die if he jumped.

"Let me finish." He turned away from the edge. "You are now and will always be my closest friend; what little I have learned in life you have already far surpassed. It's time I told you some things—"

"Cai Lun, I stayed because you are my friend. I know I never owed you more than that. If you have kept something from me, I'm sure it was in my best interest."

I could see the far western gate of Luoyang, and seven milliarium of the trade routes that stretched unbroken, all the way back to Antioch.

I turned to look in his face before he continued. "My interests were self serving…to keep you here longer. I know you want to go home. But I have also kept your payment from you." His eyes were a little misty. It was rare to see him cry. Gofu's wrinkly face darted between us as we spoke, confused about why were looked so sad.

"Payment? Payment for what?"

"Service to the king," he said.

Just as he had on our encounter in the Pamirs, Cai Lun summoned a bag of silver from thin air. Some of this man's tricks were still beyond me. The bag was as large as Gofu, twice as heavy from the look of it. I had no idea what pocket he could have hidden it in. The bag slammed to the stone in a cloud of dust.

"This is payment for the years of service. It will be more than enough for comfortable travel back to Roman borders. But I have more."

His eyes were watering now.

"What more could you possibly give me?"

From the folds of his robe, he pulled a map. "Before I found you in Merv, I heard stories of something terrible in the lands north of Rome. A group of Sarmatian traders told me the story."

He unfurled the map with a quick snap. It was a Cai Lun map alright, detailing the trade roads with intricate notations and landmarks.

"The traders told me, heading back from Goth lands, they encountered a tiny village. Damma-Ublin they called it. The village was filled with warriors. They remembered it because it seemed like a great place to trade. They said the entire town was at war with a singular foe: a castle filled with the acolytes of a demon. It was in the Rhoden Mountains. Dramatic, I know."

Cai Lun drew his finger along the path he thought best suited me, his finger landing on the terminus of the Rhoden, deep in Goth lands. "I'm not positive of the location of the castle, but I have marked the village. The traders acted like that place was the source of all evil in the world."

Gofu barked and nuzzled into his master's thigh.

"Why are you telling me this? And how could they possibly know something like that? A demon? Really?"

"I don't know, Jiu Zhu. They probably can't. What I am sure of is that this place might hold answers for you."

"Answers to what?"

Cai Lun handed me the map and turned away. Gofu looked up at me and groaned lazily.

"When you got back to Goktas, after the nameless tower, you told me that the world was harsh and cruel. You said the only way to fight was to suffer the injustice. It seemed like you laid your own demons to rest. Whatever monster set you on your journey wasn't tormenting you anymore."

I was stunned. Cai Lun was right. I hadn't thought about Bar-Abba since the tower. It was if he had never existed. I laid a hand on his shoulder, reminding him I would always be his friend.

"The time you have spent in the Han," he continued under quiet choking sobs, "leads me to believe otherwise. Every opportunity you've had, you've helped the violence of Liu Xiu and Fubo, against any better judgment. This is not the place for you. It's clear that your journey has long been in delay."

He paused. The sobs stopped. "I am sorry I hit you that day."

"…and bashed my head in." I felt the back of my skull, I could feel a raised scar from our fight.

"What you're looking for is the answer to the riddle of our time: why are men so violent? Why are we so hungry for war in the face of peace?"

His face was reddening. The exertion of holding it all in for so long was palpable.

"I lost my temper," he continued. "You have a power inside you that no one knows, not even you. I did not break you out of that prison in Merv for you to abuse that power. Be careful with what you say, what you do. People will always follow you."

"I will remember that, Cai Lun."

Gofu barked as if to reiterate.

"I'm not sure what the castle in the Rhoden is holding," he said, getting back to the point. "The soldiers I met believed their story. It might hold an answer to this question, to *your* question. Even if it's no more than a bastion of cruel men, you'll at least have sought an answer. You have grown over the years. But, your time in Luoyang has been idle. I blame myself."

He pulled my hand from his shoulder and gripped it firmly, harder than I had ever felt. I hadn't realized the well of strength Cai Lun hid until that moment.

My mind turned back to the endless road, the discomfort of life in the un-abating sun, and my long lost friends: hunger, thirst, and fear.

"Cai Lunm wait," I said, pulling my hand out of his. "When you sent me half prepared into the Paropamisadae, I didn't ask why. I blamed you when I got back, but it was my fault. I admit that now. I should have then. Do you remember what you first told me to do when we were in the Pamirs?"

"Yes, little Jiu Zhu, I know what you are going to say—"

"Do you?" I interrupted. "Well then, you'll know what I am about to ask."

My mind was racing, the threat of exile from this life of comfort taking hold. The threat of losing my friend. Cai Lun grabbed my hand again.

Neither of us wanted to let go. Only he knew it was time.

"Why?" I asked. "Why should I leave Luoyang?"

His jaw clenched. Gofu barked, sensing his master's discomfort.

"You know why. I do not want you to leave. But you have much more to do. I am not one to rob the world of such an important gift. To step into the unknown will forever change a man. Luoyang is not doing anything for you anymore. Well, nothing beyond making you a little fat," he chuckled.

I was not getting fat. If anything, I was in better shape than my journey to and from the nameless tower.

"Step into the unknown again, Jiu Zhu. Go to the Rhoden if for no other reason than to push the boundaries of your knowledge. You are not ready to return home, are you?"

"I'm not sure I ever wanted to go back," I answered. "My home is with you."

That was the first time it dawned on me. He was right. I was afraid of what awaited me at home. It's a frightening thing to leave a place of comfort, impossible at first. To wander again wasn't what I wanted, but it

114

was what I needed. I had locked Bar-Abba in a closet in my mind, sealed him behind as many doors as I could, and never faced him. I had to go home to do that. But before I turned toward Galilee I had to know why I wanted to meet the man. I didn't know why, but Cai Lun seemed to believe the Rhoden was the place to start looking.

I pulled Cai Lun into a hug. He was stronger than any man I had ever met, before or since, yet in that strength there was a profound weakness.

"I will say good bye to Liu Xiu for you," he said.

"Cai Lun?" I asked.

"Yes?"

"I'm still not sure who I am, but I'm glad you helped me look."

He smiled.

There was little I could do to thank Cai Lun. So I said goodbye with a bow and left. I closed the door to the roof, Gofu howling behind it.

Luoyang had been a warm and inviting place. I lived in luxury, and served the most powerful leader in the east. It took Cai Lun's bravery for me to realize I needed to move on. I had grown stagnant in Luoyang, but that was not why I left. Not to uncover some malicious plot in the Rhoden Mountains either. I left because Cai Lun asked it of me. I left because I trusted my friend. I did not share the faith he had in me, but I did have faith in Cai Lun.

Chapter 14

I headed back toward Anxi, along the trade routes out of Chang'an. Much had changed during my time in Luoyang. Roads west had been widened, flattened, and paved. Passage from Louyang to Anxi took ten days; it had taken weeks when I traveled east years before. Anxi had grown in the years as well, no longer an outpost but a bustling metropolis in the desert.

I took the road north, along the high plains, then west into Sarmatia and Goth held lands. This route, as Cai Lun had informed me, was barren and rarely traveled, but I needed the time alone with my thoughts. I also wanted to avoid the Kushan. I did not want to see what had happened to that kingdom, what I had done.

In Anxi, I bought enough supplies to last myself and Abraham, my new mule, a full month. I had lived nearly a decade in the city and now the seclusion of the open road called to me. True, it frightened me, but it was something I knew all too well.

The northern trade routes skirted the borders between the furthest reaches of the Han and the scattered Sarmatian tribes that occupied the Steppes above them. The road was as isolated as Cai Lun had warned, with little life but plants.

Isolation was an occupational hazard along the roads but this route was altogether different. The flat grassland and arid Steppe was immense and abyssal. It would be so easy to get lost out here; there was nothing to mark the way but endless earth. It was, at once, pristine and muted. The sense of vastness was terrifying.

My sleep was tortured with dreams of Bar-Abba once again, waking me in cold sweats, choking, gasping for air. A part of me wished I'd never left Cai Lun and the comforts of my unfettered sleep. In the luxury of Louyang, I had forgotten the feeling of an empty stomach, a parched throat, and the nightmares they brought with them. My shoulder pain flared up as well. The joint stiffened with the cold nights and ached with the blistering days. I found no bond with Abraham, as Aesop and Agape had offered. We endured each other's company, but I had never felt so alone.

The memory of my last day in Judea tortured me. The look on my mother's face as I walked out. What she told me minutes before. It was almost a decade yet as fresh as yesterday in my head.

"Ima," I asked, "...my father?"

Mom slowly turned. She looked relieved. "What is it, Zeusy?"

"Abba has never been anything but kind to me; every mistake I've made in the shop, he's patiently corrected. Every cut I've suffered from the lathe, he's bandaged. When I told him I wanted to start my own shop, he set aside some of the money we made together. I hope to be as lucky with the woman I wed as he was. But I cannot recall a single time that he has called me son. He says it all the time with Joseph, Simon, everyone else."

Her face told me before she spoke.

"Zeusy, the traveler that killed Mary's parent's, I had seen him before. There have been strange visitors in our town for many years. When your father and I first got engaged, something happened. No one knows about this."

It was what I had feared for so long, somehow already knew: "Taphas?"

"Yes... I had no choice but to allow this man to do what men will. His will was indomitable, and wayward strangers will kill when they do not get what they...what they want."

She turned back to the washing bowl and gathered herself. "*Pais*, I love you more than you know, but this is hard for me to talk about. I did not want you to know these things."

As she spoke, my anger grew.

How could I not be my father's son?

How could I be born of such an act?

I was neither angry at my mother for telling me, nor was I angry at the man who had raped her—I was furious at mankind for allowing such atrocities to take place.

"Mother, I need to know this. This is who I am...I am the son of a rapist—"

"No!" my mother interrupted in a flash of anger and then calmed herself. "No, you are your father's son. Nothing anyone has ever done will change that. Nothing you do can change that. I had lain with your father well before this happened. We were betrothed for a year before this man showed up. Your father married me after it happened to save me from our people. Had anyone found out what happened...I would have been exiled...or worse.

"Your father put yuhara aside and wed the broken, used victim of a

117

terrible crime. Not only that, he had seven children with me. We count you among that number. You are our son."

Her solace did little to quench my fiery hatred.

"Mother, did you know this man?"

"Zeusy, does it matter?"

My face grew stern as I spoke; the temperance my...father had given me was leaving.

"Ima, I need to know. Who was it?!."

"Zeus, please—"

"Mom, tell me who did this to you. Tell me who my father is!"

"I...I don't know. The time between was too short. I knew the man who came to our village. He had been here many times. Elizabeth told me he knew Herod Antipas, and his father before him...that he was the son of a priest. That was all anyone ever called him."

The pain on my mother's face was obvious, but this story needed to be told. As she relived every detail of her violation, I could feel myself changing, I could feel a hate growing inside of me, the same hate I could never muster for the Romans I now had for this man. My mother drew the truth out like an Asp's bitter poison.

"He was taller and much stronger than your father. I was alone in Savta's house at the time. I had seen him in the market before. His gaze caught my eye. I had seen that look on men before, but on this man, it was more than I could bear.

"My heart froze as he stared me down. I dropped the food I was buying and ran. He must have followed me back. I was only in the door for a moment when he kicked it in behind me.

"Before I could scream, he had his hand around my throat. He was so strong, and his hand was so large. My body froze. It only took a few moments. I can remember his smell more than anything. He did not smell like the beggars on the street. It was a smell of man I'd never caught before or since: putrid meat, the sap of pines from the desert, blood and something else...almost brimstone."

"Brimstone?" I asked.

"When he was finished, he threw me against the wall like a plaything. Your father found me unconscious. I told him what happened. We decided we would not wait to get married, that we would keep this between husband and wife. He told me he loved me and did not care how pure I was, that I was the mother of his future children, and that we

118

would raise them to be different than the strangers in our village. I have not spoken to anyone about this since."

"And his name? What was his name..." I asked, already knowing the truth was more than I could take.

"Bar-Abba."

I saw his face. I saw him thrusting in my mother, her face turned away at the horror. Then I saw him with Mary, the woman I loved. So long ago. It was Khshayarsha's face and Mithra's face. Kurush and his horrible clubs. It was Bar-Abba and the endless, dry, barren, hellscape of earth that lay before me. All fucking Mary, my would be wife, all fucking her dry.

Days stretched into weeks, then into months and what felt like years.

After what I could only guess was six months on the road—the season's change my only indicator—in the dim light of a full winter moon, my waking eyes and waking dreams coalesced into a single vision.

I saw a shadowy figure ahead of me. It was a man. He was tall, taller than any man I had ever met. Clad in heavy winter furs and skin-lined boots, his hair was thick and matted. He carried no rations, only a sword on one side and what appeared to be a small wooden club with iron fixtures on the other.

I yelled out to him even though I knew he might be dangerous. I was so lonely. He didn't respond or, perhaps, didn't understand; the man simply trudged on through the Steppe ahead of me.

I called again, this time in what little Scythian I spoke: "Traveler?! Wait! I have water and food to share!"

Still no answer.

It occurred to me he might think my voice as much a hallucination as I thought him. I dropped my bridle and ran toward him. It was almost a surprise when he didn't vanish but, instead, turned to face me.

His large face was mottled with scars, many hidden by a thick beard as matted as his hair.

Bar-Abba.

He spoke in a deep whisper, as if not to wake some malevolent beast trailing us both. "What do you want with me, filthy peasant?"

I squinted at him as though he were far away.

"Is it really you?" I asked.

"If you choose it to be...But more to the point, what are you doing here?"

We stopped walking, Bar-Abba staring at me impatiently as Abraham lazily trotted up to join us. He whinnied with discomfort.

"I'm moving west, toward the Rhoden," I answered, "to the lands above the great sea."

His voice grew harsh and booming. "And what is it you want with me?"

I fell to my knees, perplexed to the point of exhaustion with his presence. "I...I don't know."

As a storm that suddenly passes, his voice returned to a whisper. "If you do not know what you seek, how can you possibly find it? I can show you the truth. I have seen it. Something beautiful."

I stood again, the fear abated, carefully measuring his intentions. Time seemed to pass at an incredible rate. The moon moved through its full cycle. The sun rose and fell. Bar-Abba and I stared each other down, waiting for the other to make the first move.

Without warning, he clasped my throat, as he had so many times in my dreams, and squeezed. This time I didn't wake up. There was no dream to wake from. The nightmare was real. I felt life drain from my lungs. My eyes grew dark. I accepted my fate. I wanted to be rid of this world, of this walk. I wanted to go home.

At that moment, just as the first rays of light opened onto the flat earth, Bar-Abba vanished just as he had appeared. I fell to my knees, coughing air back into my lungs. My own hands were clasped so tightly around my throat they were numb. I had to peel them off, tearing my skin along with them.

I collapsed, heaving, and watched the sun slow to a stop low in the sky. Morning had come, yet again, as it always does. Abraham gently nudged me with his nose and whinnied. I took his sympathy as my cue to move on. When I stood, I was in full view of a small outpost, the first civilization I had seen in months. How I hadn't seen it before, I'll never know, but something deep inside me couldn't help but wonder if my vision of Bar-Abba had saved me.

Chapter 15

Abraham and I spent another nine months on the road to the Rhoden Mountains. After our incident in the Steppe, we grew close enough to read each other's needs. He knew when I needed to be carried, and I knew when he needed to be watered and fed. It was a pleasant distraction, even if he was just a mule. Harsh as the travel was, seeing Damma-Ublin was bittersweet. I had so craved the solitude of the open road. The threat of imminent human contact turned my stomach.

Damma-Ublin, I was here. The only Gothic I spoke was the name of the town, yet I had come too far to let a language barrier stop me. The houses were alight with torches. It was a village torn between many changing hands. The architecture showed that much. The Sarmatians had once ruled here, as had the Romans. Now the Goths had moved in, adding their own flair: ravaged, decrepit hut after ravaged, decrepit hut.

I found an inn and gave the keeper enough silver to cover myself and Abraham for a week. My plan was to gather information about the castle in the morning. I stayed with Abraham in the stable that night, for no other reason than his company. Still, my dreams were filled with Bar-Abba. What happened in the Steppe was disconcerting. Was it real? Or was I losing my mind?

I awoke after sunrise to find Damma-Ublin filled with muscle-laden Goths. The entire village was filled with mercenaries clad in armor and carrying weapons. It felt like the village was preparing for war. War, it seemed, was something I could not get away from.

I walked from the stable to the entrance where I was greeted with the overwhelming reek of unwashed, sweaty men. This inn was a meeting ground for the burliest Goths around. Most were arguing in their guttural tongue.

"Roman!" one particularly surly looking Goth yelled. "What are *you* doing here?"

Taken aback by his Latin, it took me a few moments to respond: "Sorry, what?"

"Do you want something to drink? 'Cuz it's drink or get out." He mimed a bottle pouring into his mouth.

"Sorry again. Yeah. A drink would be great."

I pulled a small coin and gave it to him. The sight of money changed his whole attitude. He poured a wood cup full of something that

121

smelled like honey.

"You want food too, Roman?"

I nodded and he walked me over to a table where men twice my size filled every seat but one. I squeezed in amongst them. Never was my stature so apparent to me than at that table. The warriors were unfazed by my presence and went about their conversation. The innkeeper returned with a tray of cheese and bread.

"You didn't answer my question. What are you doing here?" he asked, still a little perturbed.

The warriors stopped talking, awaiting my response. I hesitated to answer under the pressure.

"What do you care?" I asked with a serious tone as I lazily sipped my drink. It was disgusting. Some sort of fermented honey mixed with anise and clove. It tasted like the perfume priests wear.

My refusal excited the towheaded Goth to my right. He drew his dagger, slowly pressed it to my throat, and discerningly selected a slice of cheese from my plate. Savoring the food he had stolen—and with the knife still pressed to my throat—the Goth reprimanded me in Latin.

"We all speak a little of the imperial languages here; your rudeness is not appreciated. I'm Audamar. If you will not answer my friend the innkeeper, maybe you will answer me." He pushed the knife deeper. "As he said: What are you, a Roman among Goths, doing here?"

The two other Goths at the table took Audamar's cue and began feasting on my meal.

"Take your knife out of my throat, you northern fuck!" I said.

The man was huge, but I could feel his hand shaking. He was clumsy enough. I had no doubt I could take him in a fight but didn't yet see the point in testing him.

Audamar took another slice of cheese, pushing the blade deeper. "I will remove the knife when you answer."

I grabbed his hand and muscled it away from my neck, slamming the dagger into the wood table.

All three men and the innkeeper stopped cold.

Audamar picked the knife back up, sheathed it, and pushed a wooden cup in my direction. He grunted at the innkeeper in Gothic who rushed off. We stayed in silence, staring each other down. These men, all carrying heavy weapons, would as soon cut my head off as speak to me. I waited, breathing deeply, sweat pouring. I could take one, but not three.

The innkeeper returned with a flask. He dumped out the vile liquid in my cup and replaced it with a fresh golden one. Audamar grabbed the goblet and thrust it into my hand, his deep laugh piercing the silence.

"You might be rude, my friend, but you're brave! Drink with us," he cried merrily, slapping me on the back as he looked around at his friends. "Your business is your own. This is Burkhard and Gerhild," he said motioning to his partners. "I am Audamar. We are brothers in arms!"

All three men stood two heads taller than me and broader in the shoulders by the same. Their armor all looked the same, from the same smith perhaps: thick leather breastplates with iron shoulders and chest pads. They wore matching forest-green pants, weathered from years of life on the road. On their backs were large, wooden shields crossed with two-handed swords.

Gerhild preferred a battle spear, which lay at his side, twice his height and pointed with an iron head.

Audamar kept a braided blonde beard to match his hair, the two so long they nearly intertwined at his hips.

Burkhard had a deep, fire-colored beard flicked with strands of black. His hair was brazen and bright, sticking out from beneath a helmet he never removed.

I could not tell if they were blood brothers or had simply traveled together long enough to forge their bond. It was clear this troop was inseparable.

Audamar was the oldest and most loquacious, the quickest to anger but also the quickest to forgive, lucky for me. The others followed his lead. The three of them spoke Latin fluently, though accented with the rolling, throaty notes of their native language.

"Audamar, Burkhard, Gerhild: it is a pleasure. Now, feel free to take my cheese and bread."

The three laughed at my offer. "Much obliged," they said in unison as they continued to dig into my meal.

"You look strange for a Roman brother, what part are you from?" Burkhard asked in his rhythmic way. It made him sound like he was about to break into song.

"The provinces, south of the capital. But you already know that. Tell me, what are you three doing here?"

"That is a dark tale!" Audamar said. "Why don't you share first."

This conversation played like a lantrunculi game: I shared certain information about myself and they replied as skillfully to my questions.

"I have heard of a castle north of here and was curious," I said.

"Curious?" Burkhard asked. "Do you know what's in this castle?"

"We are after that place as well, Roman," Audamar said. "I think for a different reason."

I was sure we were all here for the same reason, but I let him finish.

"There is a...rumor that a demon lives in that awful place. He sits upon a throne carved of men's souls. He controls old evil—a power that has turned many men to a life of cruelty, torture, and depravity."

"This sounds like a ghost story," I said with a smile. "You believe in ghosts?"

"Ha!" Burkhard blurted. "This one is cavalier."

"They are no ghost, the foul men who fill the castle," Audamar continued. "The reek of death emanates from the soil, choking our land. My brother sent me here to...deal with it."

Audamar began spinning his dagger in his hand as we spoke, as if to practice his technique. The other two gorged on the rest of my dinner, leaving little for me.

"We are not here to treat with the demon," Audamar continued. "My brother wants us to destroy the creature and bring Damma-Ublin back to health. A dark cloud has fallen over the town. This may be a sign of the times, but I am not willing to accept that. If this evil were to spread..."

Gerhild and Burkhard raised their glasses to their brother's words and shouted a Gothic toast. The whole inn followed, reverberating the toast throughout the small room with loud and angry grunts.

"How far is the castle from here?" I asked.

"No more than a day's ride by horse," Burkhard replied. "It lies in the mountains above the town: the Rhoden peaks. The pass should be clear of snow this time of year, but the travel is hard regardless."

"My mule can make it; he is small but strong." I was sure I'd traveled deeper and further into any mountains than these men. If Abraham couldn't manage, I could on foot.

"Do you want to join us?" Audamar asked. He looked to his comrades to ensure they were amenable to the offer.

Burkhard smacked Audamar on the back. "Any man brave enough to walk in here and sit down at the table with our surly lot is sure to be of some use. I don't have an issue, Audamar. Gerhild?"

Gerhild grunted.

"I suppose that makes a deal," Audamar said. "Roman, you are with us." He gave me a once over. "Where is your sword?"

I had never used a weapon. Not once. I spent years abroad with thieves and generals, but I had never touched a sword. This I hadn't anticipated.

"I prefer the bow," I lied with a stammer. "It was stolen on the road. But I am sure I can get along fine without it."

Burkhard burst into laughter. "A bow? That's an interesting choice. Explains your lack of armor and small shoulders. You're going to need something though. I am sure we can find you a new bow. Come, let's go find our little friend a toy."

I shot out and pinned Burkhard's hand to the table. Now was not the time to be weak.

He laughed, throwing me off. "Alright. Alright. My apologies. Let's go find our friend a weapon."

Chapter 16

Audamar knew of a bow smith near the entrance to Damma-Ublin. The shop was small and secluded. Burkhard wasn't joking; bow craft was not prized among the Goths.

"Roman, what do you need?" Burkhard asked as we entered.

I browsed the shop, palming the first bow that looked appealing. I had no real idea what made one bow better than another. The drawstring was easy and the bow was light enough. I had to consider my shoulder. The road from Luoyang was not kind and the joint was weak. A small, light bow would have to do.

"This is all I need. Ask the salesman how much. And a quiver of iron-tipped arrows," I added. I did my best impersonation of a man who knew what he wanted. Four pieces of silver later I had my first weapon. Holding it in my hands was intoxicating. I felt powerful. I could see why Goths never let their weapons out of their sight.

We set off that hour. Despite their gruff appearance, Audamar, Gerhild, and Burkhard were courteous companions. The three rarely spoke in Gothic, even amongst themselves, favoring Latin so that I could follow the conversation. Each had their own horse, larger and sturdier than Abraham, though not as fit for mountain travel. I tried to stay behind the three, but Abraham was just too fast.

"You realize that isn't a horse, right?" Burkard commented as I pushed in front of him.

"Don't tease the Roman, brother," Audamar said. "All the Romans ride donkeys."

The nickname was getting tiring, but I was not about to correct three fearsome brothers on a mission. I needed their friendship.

"Mule, actually," I said. "They are better than horses for the mountains. And faster!"

I never had the chance to pack any new rations for Abraham or myself. This worried me, but the others seemed confident. I spent weeks planning the trip into the Paropamisadae; the four of us had spent minutes planning this siege. These three burly warriors lived by the thrill of surprise, and cavalier adventure. The three kicked their horses into full gallop to catch up. I could tell this journey would be a reckless one.

As we rode into the mountains and closer to the castle, the sky grew dark and rain began to fall in spurts. It was only midday but the sky was twilit, sparse rays of sun escaping the cloud cover. Wet weather was something foreign to me, and the lack of light set a chill in my bones I couldn't shake. My partners stared as I put on my thick winter coat.

"Where did you get that and why would a man from the south need something so hardy?" Audamar asked as he laughed.

"I needed this when I was in Kushan. I took a detour on the road to the Han and ended up in the mountains south of the Pamirs," I answered, careful not to reveal too much.

Audamar stopped laughing. "Which mountains?" he asked darkly.

"The Paropamisadae."

Burkhard looked at me in disbelief. "What?"

"The Caucasus Indicus? The mountains of Alexander?" Audamar asked.

"Yes. Have you been?" I answered.

Only Gerhild was unfazed.

"We may seem uneducated and barbaric, Roman, but we know our geography. Alexander turned his army back at the majesty of those peaks. But you traveled into them?"

Their horses panted hard to keep up with Abraham.

"Why don't you three slow down?" I suggested. "I can tell you about this story later. It might be best to focus on the task at hand."

Burkhard kicked his horse hard to catch up and ride next to me. "Tell us the story, brother."

I always hated telling stories about myself, even as a child. My mother would ask what I did during the day and nothing ever seemed important enough to mention. Thinking back, I should have been proud of what I had accomplished but riding next to these giant Goths made it seem even less important.

"I walked for three weeks before I made it to the highest points of those mountains. The travel was hard and nearly cost my life, yet here I am. I climbed about twenty five hundred pedes…"

I paused, checking to make sure Burkhard knew what a pede was. Speaking Latin and measuring in their convoluted system are two very different languages. He nodded and stowed his spear on his back to get close and hear my story.

"Most of the cliffs were sheer granite," I continued. "Getting down was worse."

My shoulder cramped painfully as I recalled scaling the nameless tower and the terrifying descent.

"This coat," I said as I plucked the warm fibers, "kept me alive."

Burkhard was in awe. Audamar's mouth was agape. Gerhild was still in the rear, picking at a spot on his pants.

"You climbed the Caucus Indus?" Burkhard asked, slapping me on the back. "I'm grateful the innkeeper sat you at our table. The Castle of Gabriel is no place for the weak."

"Gabriel?" I asked.

"Gabriel Conqvist," Gerhild replied. "He has lived in the castle for years. I am surprised, having traveled so far, you don't already know this."

"Whatever and wherever Gabriel came from," Audamar said, "he has moved far from it now. Nothing remains of Gabriel but a creature of hate. Brace yourself for his rancor."

Audamar pointed to the horizon as we rounded a curve in the trail. Standing there, a castle of immense size suddenly came into view, partially obscured by the peaks around it. Gabriel's stronghold rose right out of the mountain, hundreds of parapets, sharp as needles and dark as coal. The sky had taken on a deep purple from the fading sun and dense clouds. The features of the castle could only be seen from the torches that glowed in its many portals.

From the flickering firelight, it appeared the walls were carved from a single block of obsidian. Before the entrance, a granite bridge spanned the chasm ringing the castle.

There were no guards visible, but we tied up our horses and continued on foot. Audamar, Burkhard, and Gerhild drew their weapons. Slinging the bow and quiver on my back, I took the rear.

"Roman, you stay outside in case we need a fast exit," Audamar said. "Gerhild, stay with him until we signal otherwise. Burkhard and I will attempt to locate Gabriel. I'm hoping our tip was accurate and the castle is empty. If we alert the guards, it is your job to get us out. The men of this castle will kill all of us just for being here."

"What tip?" I asked.

Gerhild sighed and slapped his face.

"We have spies throughout Rome and as far south as Antioch," Audamar said. "We heard that Gabriel emptied his stronghold here and sent men far to the east, a mountain named Khan Tengri, leaving Gabriel alone. If we can kill the beast while he is unprotected this might be over."

128

Audamar leaned in and whispered something to Gerhild. He shook his head, swinging his beard about, but begrudgingly agreed.

"You two take position behind those rocks," Audamar said, pointing to an outcrop behind us.

I nodded, and ran to the far side of the bridge. Gerhild sauntered up next to me and shoved me over without a word. Audamar and Burkhard crossed swords before Burkhard sprinted off and leapt into a high window with acrobatic precision. Audamar followed. The blackness of the castle seemed to swallow them whole.

We were not at an elevation much higher than Damma-Ublin, but the temperature had dropped dramatically. Large piles of ice lumped around the exterior of the walls, and deep snowpack lined the courtyard. Icicles adorned the tops of the gates and the portals. Whatever was inside seemed to prefer the cold and, judging by the clouds swirling above the castle, seemed to have some power over the weather itself.

The castle, though dark and foreboding, was of incredible craftsmanship. The smooth walls and height to which they reached dwarfed Chang'an. The volume of materials needed to build such a structure seemed beyond any human undertaking, and the precision of its craftsman revealed an almost inhuman patience. It was clear Gabriel hadn't built this castle on his own. Whoever served him was equally patient and, if the stories of Gabriel's wickedness were true, as malicious.

"Where did you hear this tip, Gerhild?" I asked.

He put his hand over my mouth and pressed hard. It smelled of blood and soil. I sensed our conversation was over.

Gerhild and I sat motionless, speechless, unflinching for two hours, waiting for our partners to return. What little light the sun offered had vanished long ago. Only a dim, new moon remained. We were crouched out of sight. Gerhild was statuesque; I could not even hear his breath. After another hour, my legs fell asleep, and I stood to stretch.

"Sit now, you miserable piece of shit," Gerhild whispered.

I shot back down into position.

"Listen, you Roman fuck," Gerhild said, only loud enough for the two of us to hear. "I don't like your skinny little arms, I don't like your shitty little horse, and I don't like you. For some reason, you managed to fool my two friends in there, but I know you are no warrior. You have never touched a bow in your life, have you?"

Gerhild did not make eye contact as he berated me. I could not even see his lips move, his words were so quiet, but the hate was palpable.

"If we get into a fight," he continued. "Stay out of my way."

The clouds broke as soon as he finished, bright moonlight unveiled the darker features of the castle. Endless coiling serpents were carved into every surface, the tips of the parapets sharper than daggers, cut into the night like fangs into flesh.

Without warning, a crash rent the darkness, and a man careened out of a high window, slamming into the courtyard. A pool of blood soaked the snow. Next to the body lay a single, tall spear.

"Burkhard!" Gerhild cried, leaping out of position.

I grabbed his arm the moment he stood.

"Gerhild, stop. You have no idea what else will come out."

He lifted me up by the wrist and wrapped his hands around my throat. The pressure was like a vice; my eyes blackened immediately.

"If he dies, so do you," Gerhild said. He made eye contact for the first time since we met and poured his hate into me, as if I killed his friend. He threw me back onto the ground and ran to Burkhard. Gerhild crouched down and inspected his friend, pressing a finger into the crook of his neck. After a few still moments with nothing but the rise of smoky breath from his mouth, Gerhild rose and clenched his fists. Some of Burkard's blood dripped from his hands onto the snow. He drew his sword and leapt through the same window the others had hours prior.

Fear gripped me, tighter than Gerhild's hands. I was alone in the courtyard. There was some enemy I could not see. I had no training. Burkhard's blood spread across the snow like ink on cotton.

My certain death on the nameless tower shot into my mind.

If I could look down the blade of cold, objective death, surely I could face this.

But how could I survive where battle-tested warriors had failed? Fear and doubt penetrated all of my senses. Then it occurred to me: I could climb the castle walls!

The others had leapt headfirst into death, but there were no enemies on the walls themselves. If I could scale to the top tower, maybe the lord of this castle could be found and reasoned with. General Fubo was a man who had conquered more nations than one could count, even that man could hold a discussion. Surely Gabriel could as well.

I slung the bow to my back and tightened my boots, readying myself for the climb.

Chapter 17

The castle loomed above me.

The walls were smooth but not without weakness. The windows were evenly placed, every eight pedes up the side. Under each window was a small ledge, deep enough for me stand on and grab the next window above it. I scanned the height of the castle, careful to note resting spots. This was no different than the nameless tower, darker to be sure, but just another puzzle to solve. I warmed up my bad shoulder with forceful arm swings, and stretched my calves with a few jumps.

The castle had two tall keeps with a short guardhouse that connected them. The keeps were a stadium tall; the guardhouse was a quarter of that. All of it was built with the same black obsidian, glassy but no smoother than granite. I was sure if there were guards, they would be relegated to the guardhouse. If I could climb around it, I should be able to make it to Gabriel—or at least where I hoped Gabriel was—unscathed. I assumed Gabriel kept his quarters in the highest tower, in the keep to the right. The pinnacle there was wider. It had to hold something important.

"Well…only one way to find out," I said to myself.

Pulling into the same window the others had used was easy, acrobatic but not nearly as reckless, I told myself. I vaulted up another dozen windows, like a ladder built for Goliath. Next to me the main castle gate stretched, unbroken, the entire height of the guardhouse. It was one hundred pedes at least. Runes were carved into the wood, immaculately crafted. It looked like Persian or Haldian, but that made no sense. I paused at a window to try and translate but I was too close to read. All I could make out was, "we were always here."

Another three windows put me on the guardhouse roof. Slate tiles made it difficult to run without slipping. The guardhouse and the keeps were connected by one, giant, buttress. It hung suspended in midair, supported by some technique I had never seen. I sprinted up the side quickly and landed on the lowest window of the keep.

The first hundred pedes of the tower were caked in ice and snow. What stone peeked through the ice was frigid to the touch but no colder than the higher reaches of the nameless tower. This climb was easy by comparison. The snowpack was dense enough for me to jam my hands in and pull down hard. The climbing numbed every finger, but I moved quickly.

When the snowpack thinned, I reached a window larger than the ones below. It was covered with interwoven glass and iron. I bridged my legs on either side of the frame and ran my hand along the top support.

These windows were just as evenly placed as the ones on the guard house. I pulled my way up twenty before pausing again. The masonry of the tower was remarkable: interlaced basalt tiles ground to a perfect finish. I was grateful for the stonework. It made my sticky boots particularly effective.

I reached where Burkhard had been thrown out of in another ten windows, less than five minutes. I did my best to brush the broken glass away from the ledge before pulling up into the window. Torchlight streamed out through the broken shards, blinding me when I reached it. The interior had a foul odor of old blood, like a slaughterhouse on a hot day. This was not the place to go inside. I had to keep climbing.

Window after window, a ladder that seemed to never end. My arms began to burn, weakening my grip. I wasn't in quite the same shape I had been on the tower.

I stopped after another twenty windows and looked up, judging how much further I had to climb. The windows above had no ledge. Cut right from the stone, they were smooth and glassy as the rock around them. There was no way I could continue on holds that small. Three hundred pedes up, I had nowhere to go but inside.

What was I doing out here? What would I gain from this? Gerhild was right. I am no warrior.

Animus took me. I despised myself for being here, despised the castle for drawing me onward, despised the Goths for convincing me to come.

I was a peasant. What the hell use could I be?

The clouds parted, revealing the savage beauty of the Rhoden Mountains around me. Using a technique Cai Lun taught me in Goktas, I watched my thoughts from afar. I calmed my mind and my breathing and pushed on the window. It was cemented shut, so I wrapped my fist in a piece of my coat and knocked on the window. The glass was as firm as the stone. I knocked harder. It didn't budge. I braced my hands on either side and kicked.

It blew inward in a thousand pieces in a dramatic crack.

I might as well have used the knocker on the main gate below.

I leapt inside, landing softly on my feet, drew my bow, and strung an arrow. I had never done this before but found a grace in my movements that surprised me. It was like the weapon had been made for my hands alone.

A torch-lit stairwell curved upward and downward. I crouched into a defensive position, aimed my bow above then below and waited, listening for footfalls. None came. The castle was silent. They either hadn't heard me, or Audamar's information was true: the castle was abandoned.

Then what sent Burkhard out the window?

Releasing the tension on the bowstring, I stalked up the stairs, an arrow still notched. The winding stairs flattened onto a small foyer with a chamber at the back. I could see the door but not what was behind it. No light streamed from within. It didn't sound like anyone was inside either.

I continued up the stairs, my heart and my breath quickening with every step.

Another landing. Another door. No guards.

Another and another and another. Still nothing.

They must have had the right information, but who gave it to them and how did Burkhard die?

Something had to be here. The castle was clean but looked lived in. There were strange weapons on the floor and discarded paper pinned to the walls. Nothing looked old or abandoned.

Impatiently, I began running up the stairs. Within minutes, I made it to a final landing, lit with a crimson glow, and an open door.

There has to be something in this chamber.

I crept up to the entryway, my body low to the floor, and craned my neck around the doorway to see inside.

I had watched Roman guards crucify prisoners, had seen what the generals of the Han did to deserters. This was worse.

Audamar was strung up, naked, flayed on an iron slab. His armor and weapons were strewn across the floor.

The setting was clinical. Compared to the rest of the castle, this room was immaculately clean and well lit.

A creature loomed over Audamar. It looked like a man but was far too tall, too hairy, and too strong to be human. Covered in twitching, bulging muscles and countless scars, the thing's long, matted hair reached all the way to its calves. It wore only a bearskin around his waist. He—it seemed impossible this thing was a woman—was at least eight pedes tall.

At the side of this thing was a wooden weapon, no thicker than a club, and as long as a Roman gladius. It tapered down to a handle and had an iron fixture at its base. On the top there was a single iron tube. The same weapons were leaned against the walls of the stairs.

What is that thing? I've seen it before. On Bar-Abba!

The intelligence needed to make the tool seemed beyond the creature. This was no Persian who carved the writing on the gate.

Audamar was in poor condition. He had entered the castle only a few hours ago, but he looked like he had been tortured for days. His once proud, bright eyes were now sunken and glazed over. Blood and viscera smeared his face and beard. Audamar's limbs had lost their muscle tone as if atrophied from years of malaise, transformed into bruised lumps. The man-beast must have shattered every bone in his body and suspended him to keep the internal bleeding from taking what remained of his life. Pink rolls of sinew and muscle had been peeled from Audamar's chest, his ribs unfurled outward, exposing organs.

I nearly vomited, retreating back into the stairwell. The creature turned at the sound and shot out of the room. Without thinking, I drew tension back into my bow. The moment his head appeared, I fired, shooting the arrow straight through his skull. The behemoth fell to the stone, making only a soft thud with all the hair. I stood over the body, waiting for reinforcements to show up, and strung a new arrow to be sure. Not a sound came from above or below.

Audamar's voice seeped out of the chamber. "Roman...brother... is that you? I cannot see. Please. Please help me."

I stepped over the beast, keeping a grip on my bow. Fear surged through every muscle.

It took me some time to gather the courage to look Audamar in the face. I felt responsible. I had sat outside, waiting, feeling sorry for myself while...*this* happened. I drew in close and wiped what blood I could from his face.

"What can I do for you? How can I end this suffering?" I asked.

The brightness to his eyes returned for a moment when he set them on mine.

"Don't let me die this way. I knew you were no warrior when we met in Damma-Ublin. You have the eyes of something else, of kindness. Do me this kindness."

I stood, shocked. I had already killed one—but what I had killed could not have been a man. Killing Audamar, even if it were a mercy...I wasn't sure I could do it.

"But Audamar—"

"Please."

I could hear his rasps from two places: his mouth and his exposed lungs. They came out in wet coughs. His heart was completely exposed, out in the open, plain to view, pumping in short bursts. The shot would be easy, even for a novice executioner.

I took a step back as everything inside me fought against what had to be done, what should be done. This was a mercy, a kindness; nothing would save him.

With all my will, I pulled tension back into my bow, took aim, carefully, so as to end his pain as effectively as possible. My right shoulder exploded with fire. I was losing what courage I had. With a scream, I let my arrow fly.

With one, solid ear-deafening thud, I ended Audamar's life. As if I had sounded the alarm with my shot, footfalls immediately filled the stairs above and below. Throaty yawps shot up through the corridors. It sounded as if hundreds were moving. And they were closing fast.

I had few arrows and no courage to fight; my only hope was back out on the walls. The footsteps drew in, faster and louder. I could taste the stink of these creatures, sweat pooling in their bearskin loincloths, blood on their hands.

I aimed my bow at the window across the landing, shattering the glass with my arrow, and sprinted as fast as I could. I flew across the landing on the stairs like some sort of terrified bird. Flew out into the darkness outside and into freefall. My right hand found the cold stone of the castle walls not a moment before I would have plunged to my death. Somehow, I caught the lip of a lower window and arrested my fall with one solid, arm-tearing slap.

The creatures shouted and blared out of the broken window above me. I noticed a vertical ridge running along the entire height of the keep. A gutter a mere twenty pedes traverse from where I was.

I pulled myself to stand on the lip of the window while, one window above me, the creatures were already slinging various implements of torture and war at me. Luckily, I was protected by the ledge above as I sidled across to the next window. I made it to the gutter just as a guard stuck his head out of a window directly above me. His eyes caught mine, and he yelled in some grunt language. Something to frighten me no doubt, but my fear was gone. Only my task remained.

I wrapped my fingers tight around the gutter, smeared my boots on either side of the wall, and climbed skyward with animal speed.

This was my style of climbing: rhythmic, paced, and meditative. In the midst of battle cries erupting all around me, I found serenity.

I made the two hundred pedes to the top in a minute. The wide structure on the pinnacle opened onto another window ledge filled with a multicolored glass mural: an ouroboros wringed in flame.

I kicked in one of the lower panels and wriggled inside.

The inner chamber was darker than the desert with no moon. It smelled cleaner than the rest of the castle, but far older.

My eyes soon adjusted to discern a huge throne occupied by a man gazing at the floor. The moment I saw him, the room burst into flame, torches lighting all around us, seemingly on their own. I smelled brimstone, a smell like Cai Lun's concoction on the road to Kashi.

The man on the throne sat motionless, bent forward, his face obscured. He wore a red robe adorned with golden buttons, clothing as fine as I had ever seen, bright and expensive. His hair was straight, his skin bloodless. His eyes were pinched shut—not in sleep, but in agony. I stood entranced, staring at what must have been Gabriel. He seemed normal to me, certainly less strange than the inhuman beasts below.

Gabriel raised a palm to his face and spoke in whispered Latin. "Who are you? What are you doing in this place? What have you done to my men to excite them so?"

I kept my distance, readied with my bow and arrow. "Despite what the Goths did, I came here in peace. Someone sent me."

Had Cai Lun really sent me, I wondered, or was this the result of my own reckless abandon?

"I can smell you. Your hair. Your skin....one of the *Yehudi*...What business does a *Yehudim* have here? And what have you done to my men?" he said, barely audible.

"Your men attacked me. I defended myself."

He didn't stir. The torches burned solid, no flickering at all. I could feel their heat warm the room.

"Yet it is *you* who entered this place without permission. I ask again: What do you want with me, with this...place?"

"I came here to find out what everyone is so afraid of," I said.

"This place is my home, not a thing to be feared. I, Gabriel, am

136

the one to be feared!"

His fury ebbed and flowed like the tides, inner anguish driving it. He opened his eyes and looked at me for the first time. They were distant. Dead. I saw suffering and a longing for a sympathetic ear. I approached him, lowering my bow.

With one step I was met with blazing heat, and a blinding flash split the chamber, one quick pop like a log split by fire. Something ripped through my bad shoulder. I felt heat run down my leg. Blood pooled on the dank stone.

The pain was not immediate. All I felt at first was the wet heat of my blood. I looked down, saw a gaping hole. I looked up to see Gabriel wielding the same strange device brandished by the beast I had killed. By Bar-Abba in my dreams. Smoke rose from the end still aimed at my chest.

Then the pain set in, and the blood loss became obvious. My vision blurred and my mind hazed as I dropped to my knees.

I had gone there to understand violence, to understand why men are so quick to war. Cai Lun had sent me to the deepest chasm of darkness. How could I even begin to understand these people? How could I possibly survive?

Gabriel closed in to gloat over my body. I could see his tortured face relax at the sight of his kill. His actions and surroundings seemed mad. How else could he survive with these creatures that ripped apart Audamar? Gabriel's face became Wang Mang's. I saw the same madness in his eyes, the same loss, and regret. I saw the pathetic creature Cai Lun had seen in Wang Mang.

After Cai Lun heard about Wang Mang, we sprinted out of Kashi as fast as I sprinted toward this castle. Cai Lun's whole life had been turned upside down by that man, yet when they came face to face, all he wanted to do was forgive him.

I didn't know why that memory appeared so vividly in my mind. Part of me wondered if I was losing it, as Gabriel clearly had. I willed my mind to clear and refocused my breathing. The shroud left my eyes as I breathed deeper.

Staggering up, I limped toward Gabriel with open arms. I was barely able to stand, let alone walk, but the drive to go on, to understand, to open myself completely to his suffering called me forth.

"Whatever purpose you had here is gone," he said. "If you do not leave, I will throw your limp, dead corpse from this tower."

137

I shuffled on and forced an accepting smile to my face.

He stepped from his throne and drew a long blade. It flashed with a cold light as if it could smell my open wound, thirsted for blood.

"*Yehudim!* I will cut that limb from your body and use it to end what little life you have left."

My pace continued unabated. I was now an arm's length away. "Gabriel, share your pain with me."

The sword plunged into the wound, sending fresh new hell through my body.

I didn't allow it to register on my face. Wrapping my arms around him, I placed my cheek next to his and held him close.

"What brought you to this castle?" I asked. "I know you didn't build this place. Your story is more complex, far sadder. I can see it in your eyes. Please, share it with me."

Gabriel's hand was clenched around the hilt of his blade now buried deep in my wound. The pain was beyond what my mind could register anymore. I let go and cried.

"Who are you?" he asked, bewildered.

Through the spurts of white-hot blood pouring down my chest I whispered Liu Xiu's words: "I am your servant."

Gabriel stepped back, his eyes filled with fear, the sword left dangling from my shoulder.

"Who *are* you? Why won't you fight back?" His voice shook wildly. "Why do you push forward?" His eyes began to mist. "What do you want?"

"I just want to understand," I said.

Gabriel dropped to his knees and began to weep with me.

"I never wanted any of this," he choked between sobs. "But I had no choice. I just wanted a simple life with Eleanor and Elizabeth, my wife and daughter…but they were…they were taken from me."

I pulled the sword out and tossed it to the floor, blood pouring like a river. How I was alive, I did not know, but Gabriel's story was more important. I had to focus, but the blood loss was serious. I knew as soon as my adrenaline faded, I wouldn't be able to stand. I ripped a small piece of leather from my jacket and pressed it to the wound.

"Who took them from you Gabriel?" I asked as I joined him on the floor, my mind starting to fade in and out.

Focus.

"These men—the men in this castle—the ones all around me. I am surrounded."

He grabbed at my coat like a dog in desperate need of affection and whispered a name so inaudible it didn't register at first.

"Bar...Abba?" I asked, astonished. "Did you say Bar-Abba?"

I didn't want him to repeat the name.

Why did I ask?

"Yes...Bar-Abba...it was him, always him."

As soon as he said it again, it was real. Fear resurged ten-fold.

I have to leave.

"The men here? Where did they take your wife and daughter?" I asked.

Gabriel's sobs stopped as recklessly as they had begun, his mood shifting back to anger. "And my son!" he bellowed. "I already told you this. There is no place for men in this world. All that you love is taken from you, destroyed."

"Gabriel, I know this is not who you are. This fate is not one any would choose. And your servants are not men."

"No! They are not. They are...something else." His anger faded just as quickly, it became callous disregard. "Older, some ancient race with nothing but destruction to live for. I'm sure you realized that on your run up the stairs—or, rather, the windows."

Gabriel stood, walked over to his sword, and prepared to strike.

My shoulders began to slump.

"Gabriel, please, no. I will leave."

He pointed the sword at me. With a flash he jabbed. To my surprise, the sword point landed in a nearby torch, now a brilliant blue. I could feel the heat pouring off the light, lapping at my face like the beating rays of the sun.

The tip began to glow red-hot.

"You are a kind man, and remind me of my patient wife. She too was a Jew." As he spoke, Gabriel marveled at the slowly glowing energy in the blade, measuring, waiting for it to reach the perfect temperature. "I am impressed with your bravado and tact," he continued as the blade grew white. "You were able to scale this castle with minimal effort and came here not to destroy but to understand. I can appreciate such a feat. I will allow you to leave. But if we do not staunch this bleeding, you won't make it another step. This is going to hurt."

My voice had gone, as had my will. The only choice I had was to accept this man. Hopefully, that would be enough. I braced myself for the worst.

Gabriel removed the sword and jammed the tip into my shoulder. The pain was not nearly as bad as he had warned; maybe my threshold had already been surpassed. The aroma of my flesh cooking was sickening. Smoke rose, and the edges of the wound turned black. It smelled like pork, the pork Roman soldiers grilled at home on the streets. I always hated that smell.

I didn't struggle or scream. I just looked into Gabriel's eyes as he treated me, his own measure of kindness in this terrible place.

After a few moments he removed the sword. The bleeding had stopped, but the smell remained.

Sheathing his weapon, he motioned for the window. "I doubt with that injury you will be able to leave the way you came."

He walked through a hidden exit in the wall and into an antechamber. A new voice, deeper and more violent, boomed from behind the wall. The sound echoed through the room. It spoke in the guttural throat scratches of the other creatures in the castle. Judging from the tone, the other did not approve of Gabriel's plan. Gabriel appeared from the shadows as quickly as he had vanished.

In a heartbeat, he threw one end of a rope at me and tied the other onto his throne. "Go. Now!" he cried, pointing to the window. "He doesn't want you to leave..."

Bar-Abba is here!?

With that, I sprinted for the window and tossed the rope into the night. I jumped, nothing between myself and the snow five hundred pedes below but the rope.

As I tumbled through the night, gripping the thin cord, I could hear the cries above me, a million warthogs bellowing before the slaughter. My escape was public. I fell faster and faster, the sight of Burkhard's bloating corpse sharpening into view. Every one of these things would be running out after me if I didn't make it down quick.

Fall fast or be flayed like Audamar: those were my options.

Thirty pedes from the deck, the rope went taut, and seared my hands. Again, the smell of my own flesh cooking.

Five pedes. Two. One. With a thud, I was on the ground again, hands on fire, torso sliced open from the rope. I took off for the bridge

140

at a full sprint, clearing it in seconds.

The cries faded, the castle disappearing from sight as I moved down the trail. Sunlight squinted through a break in the clouds.

Maybe these things can't take the light. Maybe I'm safe.

I made it down into the valley before slowing. A small rabbit paused in my path, light grey and fuzzy enough to still be a baby. It stared me down to make sure I was safe, before darting back into the trees. The mother came chasing behind it.

I can't hear a thing. They must have stayed in the castle. I'm safe...I'm safe...

The sun felt good after so many hours in the bitter dark. I could see my injury in the full light of day now. It was deep; the sword had cauterized the arteries, but I could still see my pulse beating behind the singed wall of tissue. I bent to wash it in a small brook, the cool water instantly relieving my pain. I washed what I could of the blood on my clothes.

The bushes rustled.

That rabbit must not be so scared after all.

I bent down and washed my face. The rope had flaked off all over my skin, leaving a bristly coat of hemp. I closed my eyes and let it wash off.

I heard a branch snap.

When I opened my eyes, I found that twenty of the creatures from the castle had closed in on me. I didn't even hear their footfalls. The creature closest had the baby rabbit clutched in its hands, its eyes dead, the head twisted completely around. A drop of new blood splashed into the brook, swirling with the gentle current.

Fuck...

I darted up faster than the rabbit, leaping high over one of the creature's shoulders and darting away from them. They barked and turned to chase.

As soon as I cleared back onto the path I took off in full sprint. My thighs burned immediately, my heart pumped acid into every muscle. They had no need to be silent now. I heard their throaty yells move through the forest. At least ten were in front of me already, keeping pace, waiting for me to slip so they could twist my neck like that rabbit.

Damma-Ublin was only a milliarium away. I had to make it fast. If I made it there, maybe they would leave me alone. Maybe the villagers would help.

The sun was high, shining down on the alpine vegetation. A nearby stream babbled, calling to me for a long-needed drink.

No! Run!

My shoulder was useless; I couldn't move it, couldn't feel it. If I didn't make it to town…

Run!

I could see the straw roofs of the village houses. One brighter than the others. It looked like the sun was rising on that roof alone.

I smelled smoke.

A scream.

The village was on fire. Twenty more roofs burst into flame in an instant.

The walls of Damma-Ublin! They were only a few hundred pedes. I turned, and a creature was right on top of me, his claws scraping at the dirt behind my heels. Its white teeth glistened as he moved in for the kill. Drool shot out of his mouth.

I stumbled through the town gates; fires were everywhere. Hundreds of Goths were running toward the wall, swords in hand. I tripped and threw my arms up to protect myself, falling hard into the mud. The thing was on top of me before I could turn over. It pulled the same weapon Gabriel had used on me and aimed it at my head.

The same loud pop and a piercing shot sprayed across my face, kicking up dirt a hair's breadth away. I felt a blinding slap to my temple and my eyes glazed over, my mind slowed. I couldn't move.

The creature moved in close, so close I could smell its skin. Like the pelt of a deer that had lived its whole life in the wild. It was rank but familiar.

It leaned in, a blank stare over its brow. It was here on business.

Rough footsteps came from behind. I looked back to see Audamar! He had come back!

How could he be back?

The creature jumped up to fight just as Audamar jammed a dagger deep into its neck. It fell to the ground, right next to me, clutching at the metal shank with wet, choking gurgles.

Audamar stood over me, holding out his hand. I pulled on it, trying to stand. My eyes went black, and I fell hard back into the mud.

Darkness crept over me. Sleep, all I needed was sleep.

Chapter 18

In my dreams, I saw Audamar's lifeless, rotting corpse hanging in the halls of Castle Gabriel, his proud Gothic body now putrescent meat, his heart still beating. I woke up in a small room. The clamor of the battle was over.

Why is it so cold?

I need to sleep...

My dreams came back, faster and more vividly. The wet thud of my carefully aimed arrow draining Audamar's life away, repeated over and over, an endless loop. Hands gripped my throat, cold hands that seared my flesh. And words I could barely understand: "Why have you come! Where is Audamar! Speak you coward!"

I awoke again; the room was now warmly lit. An old woman stood over me, wiping the sweat from my face.

I looked over to see my shoulder nearly black, the flesh rotten. Infection had set in. The smell was worse than roasted pork. Week old cow guts. It sobered me.

"What...What is this place?" I asked the old woman. "Who are you?"

"Alfwin! Gerhude da murthra, stakka nun," she yelled in a language I didn't recognize.

Then, as she wiped my wound, the dead man who had invaded my dreams appeared, as real as day.

How could Audamar have survived?

The fear on my face must have been obvious. "Please, please, calm yourself," Audamar said, "I know now who you are. There is no need to fear me. I am no ghost. My name is Alfwin, General of the Northern tribes. Audamar is my brother. This must be confusing, I know."

He was the mirror image of his brother, but with a mature pride on his face. Deep scars snaked across his arms. This was the man who had saved me.

"I do not speak Gothic," I said.

"Friend, you and I are speaking Latin. Clearly the fever has slowed your mind. Though I hope not too slow. Can you tell me what happened to my brother?"

I took my time sitting up, pausing for the pain to slow.

"Please...Alfwin?" I asked, making sure I heard him correctly. He nodded.

"I am...confused," I continued. I turned to the old woman. "Thank you, but what has happened to my arm?"

The old woman spat on the ground. Alfwin broke into booming laughter.

"This is Hrotsuitha. She doesn't speak Latin; in fact, she hates the language. She only speaks an ancient form of Gothic. Few know it anymore, including me. I understood a little bit of the story she has told me."

The woman stood, sensing the thread of our conversation and saw herself out, muttering *"Der margund ich berdin afburn dustra nar"* as she exited.

"What is your name?" Alfwin asked.

"I need to care for this wound," I answered urgently. "Do you know what she has done?"

"I will answer your question, if you answer mine."

I was growing impatient with this Goth. "Please, this infection is getting worse." I pleaded.

"Fine then. What happened to my brother? Hrotsuitha told me she saw you leave with him and two other men in the direction of the Castle Gabriel. Judging by how you came back, I am assuming you are the only one who made it out alive. She says you cried out Audamar's name in your sleep every night. What happened to my brother?"

This was not a man to which I could lie, though the truth might be worse. I had done enough to this family, truth tempered with empathy.

As I told Alfwin my story, he grew visibly distraught, clutching the hilt of the dagger he had used to kill the creature. His face remained stoic, but his breathing hastened and his pupils widened, anger rising. As I explained Audamar's final moment, Alfwin's anger overtook him. He threw himself on me, dug his left knee into my shoulder, and pressed the dagger to my throat.

"You did *what?*"

"I did nothing! Your brother asked me to end his life. What I did was a kindness. If you want to kill me in recompense, then do it." I pressed my throat deeper into the blade and steadied myself against the pain of my shoulder.

Alfwin didn't move. I felt a drop of blood drip down my throat.

144

Suddenly I believed what I'd said: Audamar's death was no murder. I had taken the weight of that man and placed it on my own shoulders. His death was mine to bear, mine and mine alone, but I had not murdered him. If this was the payment I was to receive for such a kindness, so be it.

Alfwin's eyes were the same as his brothers, the eyes of a traveled warrior, a leader, a general. Fierce and green. This man knew the kindness of death; he had seen it on the battlefield many times. The fire in his eyes quelled.

He removed the knife, stood, and held out his hand.

"Come. Any warrior brave and foolhardy enough to follow my brother is a friend of mine."

I took his hand and pulled myself up.

"Your brother was brave but not stupid. His journey to the Castle Gabriel may have ended poorly, but the…things in that castle must be stopped. He said you sent him to do just that."

Alfwin leaned in and smelled my shoulder. He recoiled. "That smells awful."

"I met Gabriel. He claimed the creatures there were older than man, and far worse." Alfwin was barely paying attention. This man had a playful demeanor when he wasn't angry.

"They *must* be stopped," I again insisted. "They killed your brother and his men. They burned this village. Do you even care?"

Alfwin filled the room with a booming guffaw.

"Neangri, that is what the Wusun nomads call them," he said.

He walked over to the window. The village was still smoldering from the battle days before. Hammers clinked outside, rebuilding what was left of Damma-Ublin.

"Yes, I care!" Alfwin said. "But, I told my brother this fight was beyond us. He left because I refused to waste any more good men on this town. We build it up; they tear it down. Those things cannot be stopped. You aren't the first to go into Castle Gabriel, though the only I've ever heard coming out. I didn't travel this far for more violence. I came to find my brother. Now that I've found him, I need to return to the front and keep my lands free of Rome. The Neangri are no threat to my people, only this village."

I realized he might be right, hoped he was, and dropped it. I wanted to be rid of this village, of those creatures, of my fear. I just wanted to go home.

"What did that woman do to my shoulder?"

"Hrotsuitha cleared the infection and put a salve on the wound. It's going to stay black for a while. That smell is the salve, not infection. It is made from goat's piss and various...*other* things. It's woman's work, but trust me when I say it will heal." He began dabbing at the wound with the old woman's cloth. "Can we retrieve my brother's body?"

"No," I answered quickly. I had no interest in going back to that place.

Alfwin stroked his beard. "So be it. My brother's rights are precious to me, but I will not risk any more lives for the sake of tradition. He is a warrior. A warrior's place is on the battlefield, alive or dead."

Over the following days, I slowly regained my strength, and the color returned to my shoulder. Hrotsuitha's care was kind but curt. I'm not sure I ever entered back into her good graces after speaking to her in Latin, but she tended to my needs anyway.

I walked the village streets during the day. Most of Damma-Ublin had been razed from the Neangri attack. There couldn't have been more than twenty of those things, but they laid waste to the entire village. I started to wonder if Alfwin was wrong about the creatures. Were they a greater threat?

Alfwin and I had dinner every night. I told him of where I had traveled, at least as much as I was comfortable with. I told him of the nameless tower, of my time with Liu Xiu in the Han, of Mary, and my friend Cai Lun who had saved me. I learned Alfwin was the unifying force behind the many fractured tribes north of Rome. Much like Kujula of the Kushan empire, he did not wish to conquer; his sole desire was to maintain the freedom for his people. Under his strategic guidance, the unified northern tribes had kept Rome at bay for years. The stories I had heard of Goths told of barbarians fighting nude and fearless. Alfwin showed me the truth of these people, a truth far from the rumors.

I found myself greatly sympathizing with the Gothic people. Their struggle retold the same story many others faced. It made clear what I had set out to understand. My people, the Jews, had allowed the Romans to occupy our land in exchange for an increased well being, better roads, and easy access to water...but it cost us our way of life. We had little choice, as did the Goths, but the Jewish mindset allowed us to accept our fate. The Goths, on the other hand, would never accept such a fate. In the end, our struggle was the same. The Jews faced subjugation by Rome and fought against it. Some verbally, some violently, but our struggle played out between a defeated people and their masters while the Gothic struggle played out via war.

Was open resistance more effective than non-violence? I wondered. Could a conquered people commit open resistance without forcing the leash to tighten? The ever-shifting balance of power between empires was an answer to this question. Each culture answered in its own way.

Yet, the Neangri could threaten every nation equally. If twenty could destroy a village, an army of them could defeat an empire.

When I had regained most of my strength, Alfwin called me to the entrance of Damma-Ublin, the same eastern entrance I had used my first night there.

He was solemn as we marched to the gates. The sun was setting at our backs, shedding a golden, fiery light.

Alfwin held a torch. He was adorned in his battle armor, pants of the same color as his brother's, thick and spotted with stains. Bright blue mail covered his chest, crossed at the shoulders with a bear fur cape pinned with a single ruby at his heart. Alfwin's scarred arms and shoulders were exposed, bulging, carved from stone. His beard and hair were braided, creating a full helmet of brightly colored fur.

A funeral pyre had been prepared outside the gates, ten pedes tall with thick logs woven together. Atop the pyre Alfwin had laid Audamar's shield. I recognized the crest immediately. It matched Alfwin's: a white stallion with golden hair.

Alfwin handed me the torch. "I brought you here because you were the last to see my brother alive; it is our tradition that this person lights the fire to see off the dead."

Humbly, I walked to the pile of wood towering above me, a love's labor about to be reduced to ashes.

The wood had been soaked in oil—a fragrant smell of pine resin mixed with acrid tar. Holding the torch to the pyre, it exploded into high flames. They licked a spiral pattern around the pyre before reaching the top, like an ouroboros slithering around and coiling back on itself.

I stood back and soaked in the awe this sight was meant to instill. It was a glamorous reminder of life's terminus.

Alfwin and I watched the fire crackle for hours in silence. Once the pyre had burned down to embers, a fleck of the shield still glinting

147

with heat, Alfwin spoke.

"Tell me your name, friend," he said.

"Jiu..."

It had been years since I'd heard my real name. So many others had taken its place. The day I left Galilee I was eighteen. It was cool and the sun rose slow. My father and I had taken a contract from a Greek fisherman who wanted a new boat. I was carving out the center rudder with the lathe when the bow snapped and tore my leg. The blood drained so fast I almost passed out. My brother Simon had just started working with the two of us in the shop. He ran to fetch my father as soon as he heard me curse.

"Shit!" I said, scared I might ruin our contract. We needed the money, and it would furnish my new house with Mary.

My father ran in, wiping lacquer off his hands with a soiled rag. "Jesus! What did you do?"

He was mad, but not for the reason I thought.

"Simon, son, go get the needle and thread underneath the register," he said calmly to my brother.

I was doubled over, pushing hard on the wound, trying to staunch the blood. Abba walked over, gently took my hand off, tore off a piece of his own tunic and pressed the clean cloth to my leg.

"You need to be more careful, Jesus. I know you are in a hurry to finish. I want the boat to go well as much as you do, but not at the cost of your leg."

Simon showed up, breathing hard, holding a thick bone needle threaded with waxed twine.

"Thank you son," my father said. He cleaned the needle the best he could from his water bladder and held my leg down.

"Dad, I can do it!" I blurted through my controlled sobs.

"I know you can, Jesus, but I can do it quicker, and we need to stop the bleeding. Stay still."

My father's hands were fat, strong, and gentle. I had given myself a fair share of stitches working in the shop, but I always made a mess out of the wound. Abba was so fast and clean that I barely felt the fibers pull through my skin. He was done before I opened my eyes to check.

"Now take the rest of the day," he said.

"Abba, no!"

"I said take the day." The debate was over.

"Go get lunch from your mother," he said calmly. "She is having a bad day. Do your best to be nice. Give her a kiss from me. Then go see your Mary."

"Fine," I said begrudgingly.

The memory of that day flooded back like a wave. I watched the final embers of Audamar's funeral pyre smolder to a finish before I answered Alfwin.

It wasn't Jiu Zhu. That's what Cai Lun called me, but I'm no savior.

"My name is Jesus," I said to Alfwin.

"What did this to my brother?" he asked.

"A common enemy," I answered.

The moon had risen to its fullest. It shone with enough light to travel by.

I shouldered my bag and walked south for Galilee, my home.

End Book One

Book Two coming soon
The Great White Face

The Neangri and Bar-Abba are no longer at the forefront of Jesus's plight. They are now a memory, one he sorely wishes to put behind him. As he heads towards Galilee, his boyhood home, it dawns on him that there might be something waiting for him that he did not expect. Cai Lun may have been right; a task still remains, one that few others dare to face.

Pontius Pilate, Caligula, Unit Seven, and much more are waiting for Jesus as he moves slowly towards his fate, as does the promise of The Great White Face.

Check rafklein.com for details.

Acknowledgements

There are many who put time and effort aside to bring this to life. A whole life of inspiration and support culminated in this work. It could not have been completed without Andrew, Caitlin, and the friends and family that told me the truth. Yet there is one resounding facet that made this possible: all those that said no. Thank you.

www.ingramcontent.com/pod-product-compliance
Lightning Source LLC
Chambersburg PA
CBHW051836170626
46807CB00003B/1214